Jack Black & the Ship of Thieves

Carol Hughes

Random House 🏠 New York

Text copyright © 1997 by Carol Hughes
Cover art copyright © 2000 by Greg Newbold
All rights reserved under International and Pan-American Copyright Conventions. Published in
the United States by Random House, Inc., New York. Originally published in Great Britain by
Bloomsbury Publishing Plc in 1997.
First American paperback edition, 2001.

www.randomhouse.com/kids

Library of Congress Cataloging-in-Publication Data:
Hughes, Carol.
Jack Black and the ship of thieves / by Carol Hughes.
    p. cm.
SUMMARY: Having fallen from his father's airship, Jack blunders into a feud between a pirate ship
and a deadly ocean-going war machine and encounters danger, intrigue, and treachery.
ISBN 0-375-80472-2 (trade) — ISBN 0-375-90472-7 (lib. bdg.) — ISBN 0-375-80473-0 (pbk.)
[1. Pirates—Fiction. 2. Airships—Fiction. 3. Adventure and adventurers—Fiction.] I. Title.
PZ7.H873116Jac 2000 [Fic]—dc21 99-27232

Printed in the United States of America September 2001
10 9 8 7 6 5 4 3 2 1

For my John

Contents

1. The *Bellerophon*   1
2. Waiting   9
3. Above the Ice   17
4. The Central Air Shaft   33
5. A Short Walk   43
6. A Long Fall   48
7. The Thieves   59
8. Captain Quixote   70
9. The Engineer   75
10. A Challenge for Quixote   81
11. In the Hold   88
12. The Robbery   92
13. The Tale of the Fish Boy   99
14. Monster Ahoy!   110
15. The Way to Welkin Isle   117
16. Dorothy   123
17. Snake in the Grass   132
18. By the Fire   140
19. Dawn Flight   148
20. The End of an Island   156
21. The Navigator   165
22. A New Shipmate   177
23. Another Game of Challenges   182
24. Zagraff   186
25. The *Nemesis*   197
26. The Fourth Funnel   206
27. The Mountain of Snow   211
28. The Voyage Home   218

Chapter 1

The *Bellerophon*

Jack Black ran up the hill and paused at the top to catch his breath.

Before him lay the airfield with its rust-colored airstrip, wooden buildings, canvas tents, herd of sheep (to keep the grass short), and tall mooring mast. Looming over it all was the giant airship hangar. The hangar was five hundred feet high and more than one thousand feet long. It was so huge it could create its own weather, but even so, it was only just big enough to house the *Bellerophon*, the largest airship in the world. Five times bigger than the biggest blimp and faster than an ocean liner, the *Belle* was magnificent. It was hard to see her full glory, housed in the hangar as she was with men swarming about her, obscuring her with their scaffolds and ladders. But Jack had seen her when she'd been out on test runs, when the helium in her gas cells lifted her high above the airfield. Then the sun had bounced off her silver skin and dazzled all who'd seen her. She was an awe-inspiring sight, almost a thousand feet long and three hundred feet high, and, best of all, Jack's father, Captain Henry Hugo Black, was to be her captain.

Jack set off down the hill, but the sudden roar of a plane overhead made him stop and turn sharply.

The plane, a bright yellow Berger 17, shot past.

"Gadfly!" yelled Jack, waving frantically at the famous aviator's plane. "Gadfly's back!"

The yellow plane landed neatly, red dust from the airstrip rising behind it. By the time Jack reached the hangar, the yellow plane was taxiing to a stop.

Jack caught up with it and jumped onto the wing. He clung to the edge of the cockpit and laughed as he tried to pull the goggles off the pilot's face.

"Gadfly, ya varmint," he yelled at the top of his lungs. "I'm commandeering this plane. Hand it over!"

"Why, you little rotter," laughed Gadfly. "I'll teach you to go climbing on my plane." He grabbed hold of the back of Jack's belt, pulled him into the cockpit headfirst, and began to wallop him on the backside with his big gloved hand. "Putting your footprints all over the *Viper*'s pretty wings. Blunt won't be happy having to clean this off."

With an effort, Jack pulled himself upright and shot a glance at Gadfly's mechanic, Blunt, who sat in the rear cockpit bundled in flying jacket, helmet, and goggles. All Jack could see of Blunt's face was his sour, down-turned mouth.

"Hello, Blunt," said Jack cheerily. "Didn't see you there. How are you?"

Blunt just stared through Jack as though he didn't exist. Jack shrugged and leaned close to Gadfly's ear.

"Blunt wouldn't be happy if he won a diamond tiara in a raffle."

"Shhhh," hissed Gadfly. "He's the best mechanic in the world, and I'm not going to lose him just because you don't like his looks. Besides, you never know, a tiara might suit him."

Jack burst out laughing again.

As Gadfly brought the plane into the shadow of the giant hangar, Jack jumped down and ran to see the *Belle*. He knew every inch of her by heart: the twenty-four engines arranged twelve along each side, the four tail fins, the main gondola suspended beneath her belly. He stared up at the men climbing over the hull and tried to imagine what it would be like when the airship was thousands of feet above the world, cutting through the clouds. The rudders on her tail fins would shift slightly, and the *Belle* would respond by turning in a wide, graceful arc. Jack smiled. Fast planes like Gadfly's were his first love for sure, but the *Bellerophon* was special in a different way.

"How's she looking?" shouted Gadfly as he climbed down off the *Viper*.

"Fantastic!" replied Jack. "Come and see."

"You've seen one airship, you've seen them all," laughed Gadfly. He leaned against the wing of his plane and wiped his hands on a rag.

"She's almost ready for the launch," said Jack, rushing back to Gadfly's plane. "That's next week, you know. Of course you know. You're going along, aren't you?"

Gadfly frowned. "Didn't your father give you his answer yet?"

"He promised to tell me when he gets back," Jack said. "His plane should be here after tea." Jack pulled a face. "If he isn't going to take me along, I wish he'd just come out and say so."

"Jack, you know your father is a cautious man," said Gadfly, "and you're his only son. Attempting to fly around the world on an airship is no small thing. He'd never forgive himself if something happened to you."

"What could happen to me?" said Jack. "Even he says that airships are the safest way to fly. It's not as though I'd be flying a plane solo through a storm." Jack gazed up at the windswept sky. He longed to learn how to fly, but his father wouldn't teach him or even let him take lessons. Jack sighed. "I don't think I'll be able to bear it if he says no. He's got to let me go. If he doesn't, I swear, I'll run away to sea."

Gadfly laughed and threw his rag at Jack. "Your father will let you go. You just have to show him you're up to it. When he steps off that plane this evening, look him in the eye and ask him."

"Couldn't you talk to him about it?" Jack asked. He scooped the rag off the ground and wiped little circles over the *Viper*'s wing.

"No, I can't," replied Gadfly. "Come on, now. What am I always telling you?"

"You mean 'every man must make his own way in the world'?"

"Exactly, and that means *you* have to ask your father, I can't do it for you. Now, come on and help me carry my bags to the Officers' Club, and I'll buy you a beer."

Jack's eyes lit up. "You will?"

"Ha! Got you that time!" Gadfly grinned and ruffled Jack's hair. Jack threw the rag at him as Gadfly set off at a run toward the Officers' Club.

"Can't catch me," he laughed.

Jack tried, but he couldn't. He gave up and dropped to the ground laughing.

Gadfly was so wonderful. Jack watched him as he ran back, threw himself into a forward roll, and landed next to Jack. Together, they lay on the ground and stared up at the sky.

Jack had known Gadfly all his life. Jack's father and Gadfly had been at school together, and they'd fought side by side in the last war. It seemed he was always at the house having dinner or just visiting. Until recently, of course. Since Jack's father had been made a captain, he hardly ever came to visit.

Gadfly sighed. "Enough lying around," he said. "Come on, give us a hand up."

Jack leaped up and grabbed Gadfly's hand, but as he pulled, he lost his grip and flew backward, colliding with Blunt, who had come up behind them. Blunt shoved him away.

"Hey!" Jack said. He spun around and caught the insolent look on Blunt's broad, greasy face. The mechanic had removed his leather flying helmet, and his damp dun-colored hair was plastered to his forehead with sweat. A thick red welt showed where his helmet had been too tight, and around his eyes were the imprints of the flying goggles.

Jack pulled away. Gadfly winked at him, then jerked his chin at the mechanic.

"All right, Blunt, see to the bags, will you? There's a good chap." Gadfly sprang to his feet, put his arm around Jack's shoulders, and led him toward the Officers' Club.

"Just think, Jack," said Gadfly, gazing up at the sky. "This time next week we'll be flying high above the world."

"Well, you will. I don't know about me. I don't know

how I'll even get through today. Mother's having one of her tea parties and she's roped me in to help."

"Never mind. Here, this might cheer you up." Gadfly pulled a newspaper out of his back pocket and handed it to Jack.

BEAUTIFUL DARLING OF THE SKIES WINS RACE IN BETSY II, said the headline, and beneath it was a photograph of a young woman in a fur-collared flying jacket. The straps of her leather helmet hung down on either side of her bright cheery face, and her flying goggles were pushed on top of her head.

"Beryl Faversham!" Jack's face lit up. "She's wonderful. Do you know her?"

Gadfly glanced at the paper, then rolled his eyes. "Not that. This," Gadfly said, turning the newspaper over and pointing to a photograph of himself.

"Oh, can I have it? Can I?" begged Jack. Gadfly nodded. "A picture of you and one of Beryl Faversham." Jack beamed.

"Faversham's a fairly good flyer," said Gadfly. "But I heard that race she won was rigged. I hope it's not true."

"Oh," said Jack, trying to hide his disappointment.

Gadfly squinted at the sky and began to whistle the tune he always whistled when he was thinking—*Yes, we have no bananas, we have no bananas today.*

"Now," he said. "What if I take you up in the *Viper* this afternoon? That'll get you away from that tea party.

I might even let you take over the controls, if you feel up to it."

Jack stopped dead in his tracks. "Actually fly her? Do you mean it?"

Gadfly glanced at the skies. "As long as the rain holds off, I don't think there'll be any problem. You've done it before."

"Only once for a few seconds. It wasn't as though I was really flying."

"Of course you were. You can do it and I'll be there to take over if you get scared."

Jack narrowed his eyes and looked sideways at Gadfly. "You're putting me on again, aren't you?"

"Jack! Would I?" Gadfly gasped. He crossed his heart. "As long as the rain holds off, I promise, on my honor, that I'll take you up at three."

"You know my father'll be furious if he finds out I've been up in your plane and you've let me take the controls."

"Then we won't tell him. It's up to you. Remember— every man must make. . ."

" . . . his own way in the world." Jack bit his lower lip. "All right," he said, nodding. "I'll meet you back here at three." And with that he turned and ran across the airfield.

Chapter 2

Waiting

It didn't rain that afternoon, but even so Jack didn't get to fly the *Viper*. He was slipping out into the garden through the French doors when his mother caught him.

"Jack, where are you going?" she asked. "You haven't forgotten you promised to help me serve tea, have you?"

"I was just going . . . ," Jack faltered, hiding his flying goggles behind his back. "I was just going to the pond. I thought I heard a fox down there."

His mother glanced across the garden and saw the ducks waddling about calmly.

"You're probably imagining things as usual. Now come along." But as she turned him back inside, his goggles knocked against the door. His mother raised her eyebrows.

"Fox, eh? Flying fox is more like it," she said. She

pocketed the goggles and gently, but firmly, guided Jack toward the stairs. "I know my son would never break a promise to his mother, would he? Now, take your coat upstairs and then come and help."

In his room, Jack leaned against the door and frowned at the opposite wall. It was crowded with photos and newspaper clippings. Most of them were of Gadfly, but in one corner there were some of Beryl Faversham.

She looked so friendly. She hadn't really cheated, had she? But Gadfly wouldn't say such a thing without good reason. Jack smiled at the many pictures of Gadfly. He was always in some newspaper or another. It seemed that the press couldn't get enough of him, and Gadfly, generous as he was, never seemed to mind. Jack's father, on the other hand, wasn't so keen to be photographed.

Jack pulled aside a clipping of Gadfly's smiling face. Beneath it was a smaller picture of his father taken a year ago on the day of his promotion.

Jack stared at his father's face and tried to understand why he wouldn't take him along on the *Belle* or let him learn to fly. His father looked so old. His short dark beard was flecked with gray, and he already had wrinkles around his eyes. One moment those eyes seemed to be smiling at Jack, but the next they were stern and serious.

"Jack?" asked his mother, opening his bedroom door. "Are you coming? My guests will be arriving shortly."

Jack didn't move. "Why was Papa made a captain and not Gadfly?" he asked.

His mother was silent for a moment. "Maybe some men are more suited to being captains than others," she finally replied.

Jack shook his head. He didn't understand how his father was more suited to being a captain than Gadfly. Gadfly was so brave and daring. He was full of stories about how he'd fought whole battalions single-handedly and shot down more planes than any other pilot.

Jack pursed his lips. "It's good that Gadfly doesn't mind being a lieutenant when others have been made captains," he said.

"Perhaps he minds it more than we can imagine," replied Jack's mother, staring up at the vast collection of newspaper photographs. "Perhaps he's just very good at hiding it," she added half to herself.

"How do you mean?" asked Jack, but his mother shook herself and looked at her watch.

"Jack, I really don't have time for this, and neither do you," she said. "You're not even changed yet. Do hurry, please."

When his mother had gone, Jack leaned close to the picture of his father.

"Please, say I can go," Jack begged it in a whisper. "Please, Papa."

"Jack!" his mother called.

"Coming!" he answered. He let Gadfly's picture swing back over his father's picture. As Jack descended the stairs, the grandfather clock in the hall struck three. He stopped by the window and stared out at the airfield. There was the *Viper*, bright yellow against the gray walls of the hangar. Jack groaned. Gadfly was waiting for him and he couldn't go.

The afternoon passed so slowly, every minute seemed to last a week. It felt as though the world had stopped turning. No birds flew, and even the wind stopped blowing. It was as though his father would never come home.

But finally the grandfather clock struck five, and Jack saw the distant dot of a plane across the twilit sky.

Soon Jack would have his father's answer.

Jack scrambled into his coat and kissed his mother.

"Wait a minute, Jack," she said. She looped a scarf around his neck. "Don't be too hard on your father if he says no, and remember to thank him if he says yes."

Jack nodded and then wriggled away from her fussing hands and flew out the door. He charged across the garden, through the gate, and up the hill. When he reached the top, he stopped, shut his eyes, and whispered, "If the hangar doors are open, he'll say yes."

He opened his eyes and stared at the vast silhouette of the hangar. It looked so dark against the setting sun that for a moment he couldn't tell if the doors were open or not. Then suddenly, as if someone had arranged it just for him, all the lights inside the hangar went on. There was the huge silver hull of the *Bellerophon*.

Jack shrieked with joy and hurtled down the hill. The sheep scattered in front of him, their woolly backs bobbing up and down. He ran till he reached the hangar doors, then stopped and stood with his heart beating loudly in his ears. She was magnificent. BELLEROPHON it said in huge black letters along her side. The *B* was as big as a house. She was fully inflated now and floated inside the hangar like some vast, patient animal. There was only a week to go before the launch. Only a week before he'd be flying on the biggest airship in the world!

Suddenly Jack's joy vanished like smoke on the wind. What if his father said no? What then? Jack screwed up his eyes and turned his back on the beautiful airship.

He watched his father's plane land. It was a dark blue Gamworth Dragon, a twin-engine, ten-seater passenger plane. As the wheels touched the runway, a cloud of red dust flew toward the sun.

Jack felt someone nudge his shoulder. It was Gadfly, and for a moment Jack felt brave. But as he watched his father get out of the plane, his spirits sank. His father looked exhausted; perhaps now wasn't a good time to ask him anything.

"Wallace, how are you?" said Captain Black with a brief smile. He pulled off a glove and shook hands with

Gadfly. Then he turned to his son. "Jack, nice of you to come and meet me."

Jack shook his father's hand. Gadfly nudged him again. Jack coughed.

"Papa? Sir? Did you make your decision? Can I come with you on the *Belle*'s voyage?" Jack asked, his voice trailing off to a whisper.

He's going to say no, yelled a voice in his head.

"Jack, I . . . ," his father began.

It's no use, clamored the voice in Jack's head. *He's saying no!*

Captain Black cleared his throat. "Jack, I want to make it quite clear . . ."

He's saying no. No, no, no! Jack's cheeks began to burn.

"On board the *Bellerophon*," his father continued, "I'll be your captain more than I will be your father. It has to be that way. There'll be no favoritism, no special treatment, and you'll have to do as I say. If you disobey me on board the airship, it could mean a court-martial. Do you understand that?"

The voice in Jack's head fell silent. He looked up at his father.

"If you give me your solemn promise to obey every order," his father said, "then I will officially engage you as a junior able airman for this voyage."

"You mean . . ." Jack hardly dared to believe it. "You mean you're going to take me with you?"

"Will you give me your word, Jack, that you'll obey all orders?"

"Yes, sir," Jack stammered. His father was going to let him go!

"In that case, you may consider yourself the most junior member of my crew."

Captain Black stuck out his hand, but Jack had already leaped at Gadfly.

"Gadfly, I'm going! Can you believe it?" he cried.

Gadfly leaned down and whispered in Jack's ear, "I think you'd better thank your captain."

Jack turned to his father and held out his hand. "Thank you, sir, thank you. You won't regret it. I promise you won't."

Captain Black nodded and shook Jack's hand.

Suddenly flashbulbs exploded all around them.

"What the devil?" exclaimed Captain Black. They were surrounded by photographers and reporters.

"I hope you don't mind, Henry—I mean, Captain," said Gadfly. "They want to know about my part in the *Bellerophon* flight." Gadfly put his arm around Jack's shoulder and smiled at the photographers.

"It would have been better if you'd checked with me first, Lieutenant," said Captain Black. But Gadfly didn't notice the captain's anger; he was too busy fielding the reporters' questions.

"How long do you expect to be away?"

"Lieutenant, is it your intention to fly over the Polar Sea?"

"Are airships really as safe as the captain proposes?"

The photographers pressed forward. "Just another one here, sir." "That's lovely, sir." "Just another one, thank you."

"Captain Black," asked an eager-faced reporter. "Are you really taking your son on the voyage?"

"Yes, sir, I am," replied Jack's father.

Jack beamed with pride. One week from today he would be flying in the *Belle*.

Chapter 3

Above the Ice

On the day before the launch, the *Belle* was walked out of her hangar and positioned at the mooring mast.

Hundreds of people came to see her. They set up camp around the edge of the airfield and watched spellbound as three hundred men, sweating and pulling for all they were worth, coaxed the *Belle* out of her hangar. It took more than four hours to guide her to the tall mooring mast, but no one in the crowd minded. It was worth the wait just to see the *Belle* in all her splendor.

That night, before he went to bed, Jack prayed like he'd never prayed before. "Please let tomorrow be fine. Please don't let there be any storms to ruin the launch."

He was too excited to sleep. At a quarter to five in the morning he got dressed and sat by the window. As he watched the sky grow light, he thought about all the wonderful adventures he might have on the voyage. Then he smiled. The greatest adventure of all was that for the next ten or eleven days he would be flying around the world on the biggest, fastest, most beautiful airship ever built. He didn't need any more than that.

When Captain Black poked his head around Jack's door, he was not surprised to find his son dressed and ready to go.

"Come and have some breakfast," he said. "It's going to be a long day."

Jack rode to the airfield with his mother and father in the admiral's car, a burgundy Bugatti with long running boards and red leather seats. Normally Jack would have been over the moon about riding in such a splendid car, but today he hardly noticed.

The sky was overcast, and a light drizzle wet the crowds. But Captain Black was pleased with the weather. Too much sun shining on the *Belle*'s silver skin would increase the risk of gas evaporating from the cells. Captain Black nodded at the heavens. The fine, mistlike drizzle was perfect.

At the mooring mast Jack's mother spotted a smudge on his face. Before he could stop her, she whipped out a handkerchief, dabbed it on her tongue, and scrubbed roughly at his cheek. It was more than he could stand in front of his new crewmates. Jack squirmed out of her grasp.

"Here," she insisted, handing him the handkerchief and pointing to the spot. "Do it yourself, please."

Jack blotted ineffectually at the place she had indicated, and then, seeing Gadfly heading toward them, quickly stuffed the handkerchief in his pocket. Crewmates were bad enough, but it wouldn't do to have Gadfly see him prettying himself.

His mother's eyes filled with tears as she watched Jack climb the stairs at the center of the mooring mast. Jack waved to her through the crisscrossed girders. She blew him a kiss and smiled, but the smile quivered on her lips.

"Look after your father, Jack," she called. "Promise me you'll look after him."

He nodded and waved to her one last time, then turned away and climbed the steps.

Inside the airship, Jack paused to breathe in the wonderful smell of canvas, metal, and paint. He stood on the main gangway, a narrow aluminum lane squeezed between the towering gas cells that stretched all the way to the tail fins—nearly a thousand feet away! For a moment Jack felt the urge to drop his bag and run yelling with glee to the farthest end of the *Belle*, but just then several crewmen emerged from their quarters, farther along the gangway. The men were talking, but the wind moaned through the canvas and swallowed their voices.

"Move!" growled a gruff voice. Someone shoved him

in the back and nearly knocked him off the gangway. It was Blunt. Jack turned to say something but Blunt's heavy sack caught him in the face, knocking him back against the rail.

Rubbing his cheek, Jack picked up his kit bag and made his way to the crew's quarters, a narrow, canvas-walled room that ran alongside the main gangway. When he entered, Jack saw that the quarters were kitted out with low aluminum-frame beds. His was the last bed in the long row; sheets and blankets lay folded at the foot of the striped mattress. The other crew members were busily making their bunks. Those who had finished were setting out their kit in an orderly fashion.

At the bunk next to Jack's, a spotty youth with red hair was neatly folding down his top sheet. He leaned across the bed and held out his hand to Jack.

"Hello," he said cheerfully. "My name's Bill Fallow. It's my first time on an airship. It's great, isn't it?"

"Yes, it is. I'm Jack Black," answered Jack, shaking Bill's hand and then turning back to his own bed.

"I've finished here," said Bill. "I could give you a hand with yours, if you like."

"That's all right," replied Jack. "I can manage, thanks."

"See you later, then," said Bill. He pulled the canvas flap of the door aside and stepped out onto the gangway.

As Jack turned back to his work, he noticed the kit

that was neatly laid out on Bill Fallow's bunk. In pride of place was a horn-handled rigger's knife, its curved blade encased in a thick leather sheath. Jack felt a stab of jealousy. Bill Fallow was not much older than he was, but was already a rigger. He could go anywhere on the airship, even the roof. Jack's father wouldn't let him up on the roof, not in a million years.

Jack shook his head. He knew he was being stupid, wasting the day feeling envious. Jack stuck his head out the door and looked down the gangway for Bill, hoping to call him back, maybe even take him up on his offer of help, but he'd already gone. Jack promised himself he'd be nicer to him next time they met, but right now, he had to see if Gadfly had come aboard.

He found Gadfly supervising a group of airmen who were winching the *Viper* into the belly of the airship. Jack kept very quiet. He didn't want to break anyone's concentration. One mistimed maneuver and the plane could crash to the airfield, one hundred feet below. Jack leaned on the rail and watched. The waspish yellow plane with the black trim was the fastest plane in the world. She was small and quick compared to the huge, ponderous *Bellerophon*.

During the voyage Gadfly was going to fly the *Viper* out of her housing in the *Belle* and attempt to return by means of a trapeze. This trapeze was a complicated contraption of wires and hooks designed to catch the plane as it flew beneath the airship. To hook a plane to the trapeze required an incredible amount of skill, but Jack knew that if anyone could do it, Gadfly could. The *Viper* had been stripped down to enable her to carry more fuel. If the trapeze didn't work, Gadfly would have to fly all the way home.

As soon as the plane was fixed in place, Gadfly dismissed the men. He swung onto the *Viper*'s wing and checked each rope to make sure the plane was secure, then leaned over into the rear cockpit and carefully brought out a small, heavy-looking tin box. Blunt grunted and nodded toward Jack. Gadfly looked up sharply, but his impatient expression vanished when he saw Jack.

"See, Jack," he said as he carefully replaced the tin box. "The *Viper* fits perfectly."

"It's as though it was built for her," said Jack with mock seriousness.

"It *was* built for . . . hey! You're teasing me, aren't you? Just you wait till I get my hands on you!" Gadfly said, swinging off the wing and landing on the walkway. Jack bolted, but he didn't look where he was going and ran straight into his father. Jack crashed against the rail and would have toppled over it if his father hadn't grabbed his arm.

"Papa!" Jack screamed as he saw the ground a hundred feet below. His father pulled him back onto the walkway.

"Mr. Black," said the captain. His voice trembled, and he held Jack's arm tighter than he needed to. His face was as white as marble. "Mr. Black, I do not want to see members of my crew charging about the corridors of this airship. Is that quite clear?"

"Yes, sir," replied Jack.

"Be in the chart room in three minutes," he commanded. "Mr. Fallow will show you the way."

When Jack saw Bill Fallow standing behind his father, he groaned inwardly. Fallow must have heard everything.

"Come on, then," chirped Bill once the captain had left them. "It's not far, but you'd better watch your step. It can get slippery along here." He pointed down at the white grill of the gangway. "You've got to be careful all over this airship. If you fell off here you'd rip through the canvas hull, no problem."

Jack could see through the grill to the bottom of the airship. A thin strip of canvas beneath the gas cells was all that separated them from the air outside.

"Come on, then," said Bill cheerfully as he led Jack along the gangway. He stopped by a ladder that led down to the main gondola. "There you go," he said. "You'll find the chart room down there. It's the one before the control room. You can't miss it. You're lucky; you'll have a great view of the launch from there. I'll see you later." And with that Bill hurried off along the gangway.

Jack climbed down the ladder. He was excited to see what the gondola was like inside. In the chart room, he found Mr. Keats, the navigator. Mr. Keats was a tall man with hair that stuck straight up like the bristles on a brush. At that moment he was standing by a table looking at a chart that was held in place by small glass paperweights. Jack stood beside the navigator and studied the chart. The proposed course of the airship was drawn across it in a thick red line, but the chart showed only the first part of the voyage. The red line reached only as far as the Polar Sea.

"Where do we go after here?" Jack asked, pointing to the edge of the map.

"That's on another chart," the navigator said, reaching for another tube of paper. Just then Captain Black appeared at the door to the control room. Mr. Keats stood to attention and saluted.

"Mr. Keats, will you join me in the control room please," said the captain.

"Aye, sir," replied Mr. Keats.

"Mr. Black, you may come, too," added the captain.

"Aye, sir," Jack responded, and followed the navigator through the door.

The control room was at the front of the gondola and was shaped like a long, thin triangle. From waist height to the ceiling on both walls were small paneled windows, some of which were open. Captain Black led Jack to the windows in the corner by the chart room door.

"Stand here," he said. "You'll have a good view." Captain Black then returned to his post behind the helmsman, at the airship's wheel at the opposite end of the control room.

Jack looked through the window and saw his mother waving at him from far below.

"All's in order, Captain," said the first mate.

Captain Black nodded. "Very good, Mr. Burrows. Carry on."

The first mate picked up a megaphone and leaned out one of the forward windows.

"Prepare to disengage!" he commanded the men on the mooring tower.

Jack could hear the giant fastenings that held the nose cone in place being unscrewed. A moment later he felt the *Belle*'s nose lift slightly in the wind. She was no longer moored to the tower.

The first mate leaned out the window again. This time he spoke to the men on the ground.

"Drop ropes!" he ordered, and the men who were holding on to the ends of the mooring ropes threw them down.

"Up ship!" boomed the first mate's voice, and the *Bellerophon* began to rise.

On the ground, the band began to play, and thousands of spectators cheered as the magnificent vessel lifted away from her moorings and blotted out the sun with her silver, cigar-shaped hull.

Jack waved to his mother. She blew him kisses and then hunted in her handbag for a handkerchief to wave but couldn't find one, so she unwound her scarf from her broad-brimmed hat and waved that instead.

Jack watched as the people on the ground grew smaller and smaller until he could no longer distinguish his mother's face from the faces around her. Jack breathed a sigh of relief. Now it really was too late for his father to change his mind, though Jack knew he was being ridiculous. His father had never broken a promise to him.

"Start the engines, Mr. Burrows," said Captain Black.

The order was repeated, yelled in fact, along the length of the ship. All at once the *Belle*'s twenty-four engines roared into life. The *Bellerophon* jolted forward, and a shudder ran through her. Jack caught hold of a girder and turned swiftly to his father. His father showed no sign that there was anything unusual in this.

"Nice and steady," the captain told the helmsman, and the ship began to move forward gracefully.

Jack turned back to the window. They were flying away from the airfield now. He had to lay his face sideways against the pane to see the crowd or even the great hangar. Jack felt a surge of excitement. They were on their way!

Jack stayed at the window for most of the day. There was plenty to see. The airship flew over rolling green countryside, then brown and yellow fields. Jack smiled as the vast shadow of the *Belle* drifted across the patchwork-patterned land. They flew over cities, towns, and villages, over lakes and rivers, over country estates and castles. Many times people ran out their doors and waved up at the beautiful airship, and Jack waved back.

That night Jack found it hard to fall asleep. On the bunk next to his, Bill Fallow lay snoring softly, his face scrunched up against his pillow.

"Hey, Bill?" Jack whispered. "Bill?" There was no reply. Jack lay back against his pillows and listened to the comforting drone of the engines.

"I'm flying thousands of feet above the world in the greatest airship ever built," he said quietly to himself.

His father, who had just peeped in to see whether he was asleep, heard him. The captain smiled in the shadows, then left his son to his happy thoughts.

While Jack slept, the *Bellerophon* flew hundreds of miles. When he woke up, he dressed quickly and hurried to the control room. The land below had changed. It was no longer carved into neat square fields. Now dark forests with no clearings crowded around the edges of snow-covered villages. People rushed out of their houses, but instead of waving at the *Belle,* they hid in the forest. They had probably never seen an airship before and were frightened to see this silver beast floating above their village.

Far away, in the dazzle of the morning light, Jack could see a ragged coastline, and beyond it the sea. The captain gave an order, and the *Bellerophon* turned her nose to the north. Soon they were flying over the dark water. At first Jack was sure he could see white-backed whales, but as he watched, the whales rolled over and became waves breaking and melting back into the sea.

Jack was given his first direct order that morning: he was sent to fetch everyone's greatcoats, including his own. It was nearly freezing in the control room, and that was the warmest place on the airship. Everyone wore thick overcoats, fur-lined gloves and hats, heavy wool shirts, thick trousers, and long woolen underwear. Jack wore a pair of Gadfly's old leather flying gloves with rabbit-fur lining. They were two sizes too big, and he could keep them on only by bunching up his fists, but they'd been a present from Gadfly, and Jack loved them.

By the early afternoon the *Bellerophon* was sailing high above the icebergs of the Polar Sea. Jack had never seen icebergs before. They were magnificent—white and gold cliffs with deep purple shadows, destined to melt and disappear as they drifted into southern waters. Behind him, his father crossed the control room to speak with the helmsman.

"She's handling extremely well, Mr. Fitzgerald," said

Captain Black. "But I think it would be wise to take her inside those clouds up ahead."

Mr. Fitzgerald nodded and turned the wheel slightly. The airship shifted to alter course.

Jack groaned with disappointment. Flying inside the clouds would obscure the view.

"I'm sorry, Jack," said his father, joining him at the window. "I'm afraid it's necessary. Too much direct sun will cause the gas in the *Bellerophon*'s cells to expand and possibly leak out. If we fly inside clouds, we can avoid that. What are you looking at, anyway?" Captain Black stared down at the sea. "Ah, icebergs! Beautiful, aren't they?" His father folded his arms and leaned against the metal sill.

Jack stared down at the ominous dark shadows that ringed the icebergs. "Only one-eighth of them shows above the water," Jack said. "The remaining seven-eighths are hidden beneath the surface. That's why they can be so dangerous for ships."

"That's one thing we don't have to worry about up here," Jack's father said. "No iceberg will rip into our hull and cast us out into the freezing water."

"What a terrible idea," said Gadfly as he entered the control room.

Jack spun around. "Gadfly!"

Gadfly grinned. "How do you like the voyage so far?" he asked.

"It's fantastic," replied Jack.

"It is, isn't it?" agreed Gadfly, ruffling Jack's hair.

Captain Black coughed. "Mr. Gadfly," he said, clasping his hands behind his back. "When do you think you'll want to test the trapeze? I don't advise leaving it too much longer. There's a good chance we'll run into some bad weather once we get farther north."

Gadfly glanced at the sky. "I was just coming to ask you about that, sir. Blunt has found some very minor problems with the *Viper* but thinks we should be ready to make our first sortie within the next few hours. With your permission, of course." Gadfly looked at his wristwatch. "Certainly no later than sixteen hundred hours?"

Captain Black nodded. "Very good," he said. "Check back with me before you set up, in case there's been a turn in the weather."

"Aye, sir," Gadfly said. He saluted, winked at Jack, then left the control room.

Jack smiled and returned to the window. He thrust his hands into his pockets and scrunched up his fists inside his gloves, delighting in the feel of soft rabbit fur between his fingers.

The airship entered the clouds. The pale white wisps whipped past the window, gradually becoming so thick that Jack could no longer see the sea.

For the next half hour he sat in the chart room watching Mr. Keats at work and listening to the thrum of the engines. Then Jack overheard his father give an order in the control room.

"Mr. Fitzgerald, bring her up so that Mr. Keats can take a reading," the captain said.

Jack looked up as his father appeared at the chart room door.

"Can I go with Mr. Keats, sir?" asked Jack.

Captain Black fixed Jack with a stern eye. "You can go as far as the air shaft," he said. "But you must wait on the gangway. No climbing!"

"But you know how well I can climb," Jack said. "I'll be all right. . . ."

The look on his father's face commanded him to stop. "Did you hear my order, sir?" said the captain. "You are to wait on the gangway."

"Yes, sir," mumbled Jack.

"Here, Jack," said the navigator, handing him a brown leather case. "Carry the sextant for me, will you?"

Jack took the case and, ducking his head, looped the long strap across his body. Carrying the ship's sextant wasn't nearly as exciting as climbing the air shaft and taking a reading, but it was still important. Jack pursed his lips. He would just have to be satisfied with that.

As Jack started up the ladder to the main gangway, he heard his father call, "Mr. Black, promise me, no climbing!"

"Yes, sir," he answered without looking back.

Captain Black stared at the ladder for some time after Jack had gone. He shook his head and wondered if he'd done the right thing in bringing him along. But the boy had so wanted to come, and Captain Black was not so old that he couldn't remember how it felt to want something that badly.

Chapter 4

The Central Air Shaft

In the stillness of the hangar, the *Belle*'s main gangway had been a straight, narrow aisle between the gigantic gas cells. But now that she was flying and twisting in the wind, the gangway became a constantly winding and unwinding path. Although the navigator was only a few feet ahead of Jack as they made their way to the central air shaft, he would sometimes vanish from sight behind a gas cell as the gangway twisted, only to reappear moments later as it straightened out.

There were seven air shafts spaced evenly along the body of the *Belle*, but the best one from which to take a reading was the fourth. The camber of the top of the hull made it the highest point on the ship.

When they reached the central air shaft, Jack lifted the sextant case from around his neck and handed it to

Mr. Keats. The navigator took it and, climbing the ladder, disappeared up the shaft. He had been gone only a few moments when the corridor in front of Jack straightened out and he saw an airman hurrying toward him. It was Bill Fallow, and his face was as white as wax.

"Is there an officer about?" stammered Bill. He was cradling his left hand in his right, and the sleeve of his uniform was black with blood. "Caught it with my own knife," he said. "Stupid!"

Jack stared at a gash that ran right across Bill's palm. It was a bad cut, deep and gaping; his hand was sliced almost to the bone. Bill slumped against the rail. He looked as if he was about to faint. "Please, get someone," he hissed through gritted teeth.

Jack drove back feelings of nausea and forced himself to look away from the ugly red wound. "Hold on," he said. He craned his head back and called up into the air shaft, "Mr. Keats! Mr. Keats!"

Jack could see the navigator at the top of the ladder two hundred feet above. He already had his head and shoulders through the hatch. He wouldn't be able to hear Jack shouting.

Jack took hold of the ladder, climbed the first couple of rungs, and called again. There was still no reply. He would have to climb up and bring the navigator down. The promise he'd made to his father flashed through his mind. He knew he shouldn't break his word, but this was an emergency. Jack glanced at Bill Fallow's ashen face. Surely his father would understand.

"Sir!" he called as he hurried hand over hand into the darkness of the shaft. "Mr. Keats!" Climbing the ladder was easy, and in no time Jack had reached the top.

"Sir!" he shouted, tugging on the navigator's trouser cuff. The navigator ducked his head down out of the wind.

"What are you doing up here?" said Mr. Keats. "I haven't finished yet. What is it?"

When Jack told him about Bill's accident, the navigator acted swiftly. He put the sextant and notebook back in the case and hurried down the ladder after Jack.

"It's a nasty cut," said Mr. Keats, looking at Bill's hand. "I'll take him to get it stitched up." Bill groaned. The navigator handed the sextant case to Jack.

"You wait here till I return," he said. "I haven't taken the reading yet. I'll be back in a few minutes."

Keats led Bill away, and they disappeared behind a twist in the corridor. Drops of blood glistened on the white metal floor. Jack winced and looked away, then leaned back against the ladder.

As he waited he heard a strange noise. It was a sort of whistling, but it wasn't high pitched like most whistles; it was deep and musical. It sounded like someone blowing across the top of a bottle. Jack tipped his head back and looked up the shaft. The navigator had left the hatch open—the wind blowing across the open shaft was making the noise. More than anything Jack wanted to climb up and poke his head into the clouds. What did the world look like from up there? Jack tore his eyes away. He'd promised his father he wouldn't climb. He'd been told not to. It was more than his father's request, it was an order from his captain. He'd given his word that he wouldn't.

But he'd been up there once, so he'd already broken his promise to his father. What difference did it make now? Jack craned his head back. He already knew he could do it. The climb was a piece of cake, not dangerous at all. The wind moaned louder, and Jack imagined that it was calling to him, urging him on. "Come and see," it seemed to be saying. "Come and see."

Jack grasped the ladder with both hands and set his foot on the first rung. His father would be angry, but how would he ever find out? Who would tell him? Jack stared up at the sky. Now the wind was whispering Gadfly's favorite saying. "Every man must make his own way in the world," seemed to echo down the shaft. "Every man must make his own way." Jack knew exactly what Gadfly would expect him to do.

He peered along the twisting corridor in both directions. There was no one around. The navigator would return soon, but Jack didn't need long. He would climb to the top, look out, and come down again. No one would ever know. Jack took a deep breath and started to climb as fast as he could.

At the top he pulled his goggles over his eyes, adjusted his gloves, and let the roaring wind drown out his nagging conscience. He took another deep breath, stuck his head through the hatch, and gasped.

Nothing had prepared him for the thrill of riding through the sky. It was incredible. For the navigator to be able to take the reading, Captain Black had brought the airship just high enough for a man's head to stick above the clouds, while the rest of the airship remained hidden beneath. Jack laughed as the clouds swirled around him, and the strong blustering winds snatched his laugh away.

For a moment the *Belle* emerged through the clouds like a great silver whale breaching in a foaming white sea. Her silver skin glittered with frost. Jack reached out and touched it. His finger slipped away. It would be madness to try and walk on the hull. He thought of the riggers who would have to do it during the course of the voyage and shuddered.

The *Bellerophon* dipped her nose and disappeared from sight once more. The airship sailed smooth and steady. In the far distance the clouds were tinged with gray as though polluted by some enormous fire. It looked like a storm up ahead.

If there's a storm coming, I'd better take a reading now,

Jack thought, forgetting, as he undid the clasp on the case, that he wasn't even supposed to be up there, let alone handling the sextant, the airship's precious navigational tool. They had only one and if that got lost they wouldn't be able to find their way home.

Very carefully Jack took out the sextant and slipped his wrist through the holding strap. He put the telescope to his eye and carefully moved the index bar until the sun appeared to sit on the artificial horizon. This done, he took out the notebook and pencil—it was important to make a record of the reading. But the wind almost snatched the notebook out of his hand, and, as he made a grab for it, he let go of the sextant. It bounced against the hull. If it hadn't been for the wrist strap, it would have fallen.

Jack was shaking as he ducked down inside the shaft. He closed the sliding hatch over his head and wedged himself against the narrow walls. Though the wind still moaned above him and the ship still creaked and groaned, it was much quieter with the hatch closed. His goggles were all steamed up, so he pushed them onto his forehead. He opened the notebook to a clean page and jotted down the reading. Then he made a note of the exact time, 13:16, and the date, the twenty-third of April.

A dewdrop fell from the end of his nose, smearing the figures on the page.

"Drat!" he said, scrabbling in his overcoat pocket to find something to clean up the mess. To his surprise he pulled out his mother's dainty lace-trimmed handkerchief. He blotted the page, closed the notebook, and returned it with the sextant to the case. Then he wiped his nose. The handkerchief smelled so strongly of his mother's perfume that he was almost overcome with homesickness. For the first time since he had left the ground, he was glad that he would be home in a week or so.

. As he sat there thinking of his home and listening to the raging echoes of the wind, he became aware of a new sound, separate from the wind and yet seeming to belong to it. It was horribly distorted as if full of static, like a voice on a badly tuned radio. Jack held his breath and listened.

"The good Captain Black, ha! I'll give him his rank," the voice hissed. "I'll give him his respect. . . ."

Jack twisted around. No one could be in the shaft with him, it was impossible. There wasn't room! Jack shook his head. It was just the wind howling through the airship; it was just distortion in the distant drone of the engines. Then he heard it again.

"Did you fix the rudder like I told you?" asked the voice. "Will they be able to set her back on course?"

"Nah, it's as tight as a cork in a bottle," replied another voice. "They won't feel a thing in the controls, least not till it's too late. They'll be good and lost when they come down. I fixed the rudder when I was up there with the bomb. . . ."

Jack sat up like a startled rabbit. A bomb? Someone had set a bomb on board the *Belle?* He had to warn his father! Jack held his breath and crouched forward, trying to hear more, but the wind had swallowed up the voices. He cupped his hands around his ears and listened carefully.

". . . the tail fin . . ."

". . . sixteen hundred hours . . ."

The bomb was set to go off in less than three hours! There were four tail fins, and each one was over ninety feet long. If what he heard was true, there was no time to lose.

The wind died, and the voices began hissing and crackling again.

". . . make sure the navigator doesn't get a chance to take his reading. You wait here and distract him some-how. Better still, find a way to get that sextant off him. We don't want anyone else knowing where she comes down."

"But . . ." The other voice sounded nervous. "What if the airship doesn't come down? What if she explodes?"

"I've told you, she won't explode," replied the first voice. "She's filled with helium—it's nonflammable. She's just going to float down, nice and gentle. Come on, man, you're being paid enough, aren't you? Just make sure it looks like sloppy sailing on Black's part."

Suddenly the wind screamed down the shaft, momentarily drowning out the voices. Jack strained his ears.

". . . you watch out for Keats," hissed the voice. "And I'll get the *Viper* ready."

Jack jumped. The saboteurs were going to use the *Viper* to escape. He had to warn Gadfly! He looked down the shaft toward the gangway, but a man was standing at the bottom, blocking his escape. With a shock Jack recognized the man's thinning dun-colored hair.

"Blunt!" he gasped. Blunt was plotting to blow up the *Belle!*

Jack had to get to Gadfly or his father and tell them what he'd heard, but how was he going to get to them when Blunt blocked his way?

"Go away. Move!" Jack hissed under his breath. But Blunt didn't budge. He seemed to have taken root.

Jack glanced up at the hatch. There was another way of getting to his father. He could climb across the top of the hull and down the next air shaft, but that meant a difficult crawl of one hundred feet or more across the icy hull. Jack bit his lip. It was dangerous. He shifted in his seat and his mother's lace handkerchief slipped from his lap. Jack tried to catch it, but it fell too fast. He watched in horror as it floated to the bottom of the shaft, a lacy messenger of betrayal swish-swaying toward Blunt's head.

Now he had no choice. If he stayed where he was, Blunt would find him like a rabbit in a hole. Jack threw open the hatch, grabbed one of the steel guide ropes, and pulled himself onto the hull.

Chapter 5

A Short Walk

On the top of the hull the wind was fierce and biting. Jack pulled himself out of the air shaft and lay on his belly as the clouds rushed over him. He could just make out the dim hump of the next air shaft's cover. It was a hundred feet away toward the *Belle*'s nose. Jack's teeth chattered, and the ice-covered rope burned through his fur-lined gloves.

He lifted himself to his knees and, keeping a firm hold on the rope, began to creep forward. It was a slow, torturous crawl through the swirling clouds, pulling himself along by inches, with his knees threatening to slip away from him at every step.

He was halfway across when he saw Blunt's head appear out of the air shaft—in front of him! Jack flattened his body against the canvas and pressed his face against the icy hull, praying that the clouds would keep him covered.

He knew he couldn't stay where he was for long. Blunt would soon find him cowering in the clouds. He tried to retreat on his belly, but he moved so slowly that Blunt would soon catch up to him. He had to get out of Blunt's path, and that left him with only one choice. He'd have to lower himself down one of the ropes that ran around the belly of the airship. These were the ropes that the senior riggers used if they had to make repairs during a flight. Jack knew it was a crazy idea, but he had no alternative.

He reached for one of the ropes, took a firm hold, and swung down. Now, at least, he was out of Blunt's path. As long as the clouds covered him, he was safe, but the clouds were getting thinner. Looking up Jack could see Blunt through the racing white mists. Jack lowered himself even farther down the hull. How long, he wondered, could he hold on?

Then the airship passed into clear skies, and the clouds fell away. Thousands of feet below, the icebergs raised their jagged peaks to heaven. To the north, the storm clouds that Jack had seen from the top of the hull were growing darker. He could hear the distant boom of thunder and knew he wouldn't have a chance of clinging to the hull if the *Belle* flew through a storm.

"Jack! Jack, are you all right?" It was Gadfly's voice.

"Where are you, Jack? What the devil are you playing at? Blunt saw you climb up here and came to fetch me. Jack, don't you realize how dangerous this is?"

Jack looked up and saw Gadfly standing on the hull with the sun shining all around him. Mr. Keats stood behind him. Suddenly Jack felt much better. Gadfly would make everything all right.

"Gadfly, help!" he cried.

Gadfly looked down and saw Jack disappearing around the curve of the *Belle*'s hull. "Good God, Jack!" he cried. He got down on his knees, lay on his stomach, and reached a hand toward Jack. "Hold on, we'll get you," he said. "Blunt! Take hold of my legs. Keats, tie a rope to Blunt and wedge yourself in the air shaft. Try and keep it steady. Jack, hold on. I'm coming down."

"Gadfly, I was trying to get to my father," Jack explained. "I heard . . . there was someone talking about a bomb . . . about blowing up the airship!" Jack's voice fell to a half-whisper. "I'm sure it was . . . Blunt. He's put a bomb on one of the tail fins!"

"Jack, save your breath," Gadfly said, struggling to reach him. "You can tell me everything when you're safe. Come on, reach up. Just a little farther."

"They're going to steal the *Viper* to get away," Jack said.

"Concentrate, Jack!" Gadfly snapped. "Here, quick, grab my hand." Gadfly's fingers were just a few inches away. Jack strained to reach them, his feet scrabbling against the slippery hull. His grip on the icy cable slipped. With a cry Jack glanced down at the cold sea thousands of feet below.

"Hang on, Jack," urged Gadfly through clenched teeth. "Just an inch more. Come on."

With one almighty effort Jack forced himself another couple of inches up the vertical ropes. It was just enough.

Gadfly lurched forward as he took Jack's weight. Blunt lurched, too. In the air shaft, Mr. Keats tightened the rope across his shoulders and wedged himself in more firmly.

"It's all right," puffed Gadfly. "I've got you. Come on; easy now. Steady there, Blunt."

Jack's arm felt like it was going to be pulled out at the root. He scrabbled with his feet, trying to get a toehold on the hull.

Then Gadfly started to slip. It was as if Blunt couldn't hold the weight of both Gadfly and Jack.

"Jack, the angle's too steep, and you're too heavy to pull up," grunted Gadfly. "If you could get rid of your greatcoat, we'd have a better chance. You'll have to lift the sextant off first."

Jack's head throbbed, and the intermittent boom of the approaching thunder pounded in his ears. His arm was aching so much now that he had to bite his lip to stop from crying. It would be the end if he cried in front of Gadfly.

"Okay, Jack, pass the sextant up to me," Gadfly said. "Come on. Just lift it over your head. Then you can get your coat off, and we'll have you up in no time."

Jack had forgotten about the sextant. It was still looped across his body. Of course, Gadfly was right. Jack couldn't take off his greatcoat without removing the sextant case first. With his free hand he started to loop the strap over his head. He'd almost done it when he felt the hand Gadfly was holding begin to slip inside his loose glove. His fingers were so numb that he could do nothing to stop it. He turned his terrified eyes from Gadfly to Blunt. A thin flicker of a smile crinkled Blunt's thick lips. Jack gasped, and his hand slipped another notch.

"Jack, hold on!" Gadfly said. "Don't let go, Jack. Pass me the sextant. Pass me the sext—" But it was too late. Jack's hand slipped out of the glove like a whisper, and he fell.

"Gadfly!" he screamed as Gadfly's face vanished over the curve of the hull.

"Jack!" cried Gadfly. *"Damn! Damn! Damn!"*

Chapter 6

A Long Fall

For the first few moments it seemed to Jack as though he weren't falling at all. Tiny details on the hull became crystal clear. He could see each crisscross stitch, and even the weave of the canvas. His father stood at the window of the control room, but he was not looking in Jack's direction.

"*Papa!*" cried Jack. And as he cried, the world returned to its proper speed. The *Belle* shot up into the air, and Jack plummeted toward the sea.

Once away from the shelter of the airship, the winds made light work of him. They threw him one way, then snatched him up and threw him another.

I'm going to die, Jack thought as he spun through the air with his greatcoat swinging out about him. *Oh, God, please let me fall quickly*. But the winds wouldn't let him go. They blew him toward the storm he had seen from the top of the airship. The swirling black clouds drew him in, and the persistent thunder roared in his ears.

It was the strangest, darkest storm Jack had ever seen. The clouds were rank and sooty. The thick air scratched his eyes, and he could hardly breathe. Violent flashes of fire exploded in the void beneath him and illuminated the blackness with an eerie orange light. Enveloped in the thick dark clouds, Jack no longer had any sense of what was up or down.

Suddenly there was a burst of fire far larger and closer than the others. Within moments Jack was on the other side of the storm and out in the clear sky, falling again toward the sea.

Behind him the thick clouds still churned and billowed, but now, as he turned over in the wind, Jack could see that this was no storm. The clouds were clouds of smoke, and they were rising from the funnels of an enormous warship.

The warship rose out of the water like a dark windowless city, a thousand feet high. Bright arcs of blue lightning fizzed and crackled up her two gigantic radio masts. Her hull was streaked and mottled with corrosion. Orange rivers discolored her steep sides, and hundreds of guns swiveled in rusted turrets. For all this, her seven great funnels stood proud and straight—a line of ancient monoliths, massive, immovable, indestructible. Each funnel bore the remains of a red enamel letter much worn away by the sharp salt air; together, they spelled— NEMESIS.

"The *Nemesis*," Jack said to himself.

The great iron monster plowed through the sea, the black clouds from its funnels trailing behind it like a widow's veil. The warship was chasing a small schooner-rigged steamship through the ice-encrusted waters. The warship fired again and again, and as the shells exploded, their fire lit up the sky. The little ship dodged and darted out of the way of the fearsome artillery, and even as she fled across the waves, she had the pluck to fire back. But her guns were useless against such a massive opponent. Her best efforts didn't even make the smallest dent in the great ship's iron sides.

All would soon be over for the little ship. She was trapped against the ice with the shells from the warship thundering all around her. The noise was terrible. The explosions shook the air and fought with the wind to blow Jack about.

Then the tiny ship reversed away from the ice and turned to face the warship, heading straight toward the massive bow: a wood-hulled David against an iron Goliath. Jack closed his eyes—the steamship would be crushed like a snail beneath a wheel.

A volley of infuriated blasts from the big guns sent Jack reeling. Then, suddenly, the firing stopped.

Miraculously, the little ship had slipped along one side of the great cleaver bow; it now sailed a hairbreadth away from the mighty hull. The great guns clanged angrily against the lower rim of their turrets; they could not fire straight down. As long as the little ship stayed close to the warship's hull, she was safe. But she couldn't stay there forever.

Suddenly the huge guns began to roar again, and the wind picked Jack up and then dropped him hundreds of feet. The icy water rose quickly to meet him. Jack screamed once, then lost consciousness.

It was lucky for him that he did. Had he been aware of his amazing luck, things might not have turned out as well as they did.

Jack was only a hundred feet from the water when a blast from a last exploding shell turned him around and sent him reeling across the sky. At this very moment the schooner, to avoid scraping her hull against an iceberg, changed direction sharply and found herself running down between two towering waves—an almost vertical drop into a gray valley of water. As she came around in the darkest part of the valley, her fore topsail caught a breath of wind and with it, the limp body of a boy. The sail scooped Jack out of the air, like a father catching a baby.

Jack slid down that sail and bounced onto the one below, which caught him just as gently as the first. From there he slid onto the foresail, which cast him out onto the deck with such force that he tore a hole in the rotted roof of the forecastle. Falling right through, Jack landed on a heap of sopping blankets and filthy clothes that were strewn across a wildly swinging hammock.

The little ship darted out of the shadow of the warship, twisting and turning to avoid the shells from the *Nemesis*. With her sails full and her engines straining, she cut over the water and raced away. The *Nemesis* chased her all the way to the edge of a storm, where lightning flashed and the sea rolled mountains, but once the little ship entered the stormy waters, the *Nemesis* did not follow. At the first flashes of lightning the mighty warship slowed and turned away.

In the forecastle, Jack knew nothing of his miraculous landing. In his mind, he was back at home in his own bed, and the only thing to bother him was a cold hot-water bottle at his feet. He groaned and kicked in his unconscious state until, believing that he had dislodged the offending bottle, he snuggled down to sleep.

His dreams rambled, shifting and changing like dunes in the wind. Beryl Faversham, with her bright happy smile, was tying a bomb to the tail of the airship and blowing kisses to Blunt. Jack flew in the *Viper*, looping loops around the airship as it dropped slowly out of the sky. Gadfly was laughing and running along the top of the *Belle*. He was splashing through the deep puddles that had somehow formed in the hollows as the airship deflated and dropped toward the sea.

With a gasp Jack opened his eyes. At first he saw nothing but a fuzzy blackness spotted with a strange, dappled light. And there was the foulest smell. . . .

I'm blind! he thought, bringing his hand to his face. A thick woolen sock lay over his eyes. Jack pulled it away quickly.

He tried to get up, but the hammock swayed violently beneath him and threatened to pitch him out. Jack didn't want to fall out of anywhere; he'd had enough of that to last him a lifetime. Carefully he lifted his head and peered into the dismal room. A lamp hung above a rough wooden table. Around it, motley canvas hammocks were slung from the rafters. They swayed in time with the lamp. Low wooden bunks full of dirty rags and blankets lined the walls three high. The floor was wet. Seawater slopped back and forth, lapping at the walls in waves.

I'm on a ship, thought Jack. *But what kind of ship is this?*

Everywhere there was the rank smell of moldy cheese and boiling sugar all mixed together, a nauseating smell. Jack slumped back into the hammock. He felt as if he were one big bruise from head to toe. He turned his nose in the direction of the roof and looked at the pale sky through the ragged hole above him.

The room rocked and the hammock swayed, and the sound of the sea cradled him back to sleep.

§

The forecastle door burst open and crashed against the wall. Jack woke with a jolt. The sky was dark. He peeped over the edge of the hammock and silently drew a stinking blanket over his head, taking care to leave a narrow slit to see through.

Four men entered the dimly lit room. Jack shuddered as they crossed into the light. Each haggard face was meaner than the last. Their brows were set in terrible frowns and their mouths were hard and grim. Two of them wore eye patches. As they sat down at the table, their daggers and pistols clanked against the wooden benches.

Jack shrank beneath the blanket. Everything about these men confirmed his worst fears. This had to be a pirate ship. No respectable vessel would have such men on board.

How long? he wondered. *How long before I'm discovered? How can I escape?* And, not for the last time, he deeply regretted climbing up the air shaft.

The door opened again, and a young fellow, so tall that he could hardly stand up in the low-beamed room, entered carrying a tray of mugs and a plate piled high with thick slices of bread and butter. He set his tray on the table, and the men pounced on the food like animals. Within seconds the plate was empty and each man's mouth was full.

Then the stern-faced man nearest the door thumped

his fist down on the tabletop, making the plates rattle. He waited till he had everyone's attention, then lifted his mug high.

"A toast to the *Hyperion,* our miracle ship. God bless her for saving our souls yet again."

"Aye, Eric Lamb, bless her, indeed!" agreed the rest, clinking their mugs together. "Heaven keep her safe."

The stern-faced man continued. "I thought we were done for this time. When we saw the you-know-what on the horizon, I heard Captain Quixote curse that name he always curses. . . ."

"Gregor Ladislav Lavinovich," growled one of the others.

"Aye, that's it, Thomas." Eric Lamb paused and took a deep draft from his mug, then lowered it to the table and stared into space. "When I saw that vile warship bearing down on us, the blood ran cold in my veins. If we hadn't escaped into that storm with all the speed this miraculous ship can muster, we'd have been . . . well . . . All I can say is thank heaven for the storm where that warship would not follow. For all its mighty huff and puff, I think it fears the lightning." The men around the table laughed. "The storm was bad enough," continued Eric Lamb, "with its hailstones as big as our fists and the wind blowing fit to tear holes in our heads, but I'm telling you, I would rather ride that storm seven times over than face the *Nemesis* again."

The others shifted uncomfortably in their seats.

"Watch what you say, Eric Lamb," hissed one man.

"Simon's right," hissed another. "You know what Quixote'd do if he heard you."

The grim-faced men fell silent, and only the creaking of the ship's timbers and the roar of the sea could be heard.

Suddenly the tall lad cried out, "Mr. Lamb? Mr. Lamb? Was the ship . . . was it . . . Well, were we hit? Did any of the shells hit us?"

The men burst out laughing. The boy blushed.

"Sky, lad," snorted Eric Lamb. "If we'd been hit by one of those shells, I don't think we'd be sitting here having our tea. We'd be signing up with Davy Jones or Saint Peter or someone."

Sky pressed his point. "It's just that . . . well . . . where did that hole come from?"

Everyone turned and looked. The gray light of dawn filtered through the hole that Jack had made. Jack ducked down, but he moved too quickly and the hammock began to sway. The more he tried to stay still, the more it moved.

"That's odd," said Eric Lamb as he watched the one hammock swinging out of time with the others. "Could be a rat. Sky, go and catch it. Hurry, lad, see what it is."

Tentatively Sky approached the swinging hammock. Twice he stopped and turned around. "It's not a rat," he said. "A rat'd make some noise. It's something peculiar. I don't like it."

"Get on with it," muttered Tom. Sky crept reluctantly toward the hammock. He stopped again.

"Go on, it won't bite you," Simon sniggered, knowing full well that if it was a rat, it might.

Buried deep within the tangle of clothes, Jack tried not to breathe too loudly. The musty stench made it hard to breathe at all. He could hear Sky's hesitant step across the creaking boards. Jack willed the hammock to stay still, but it just rocked on.

Sky grabbed a broom. He leaned over and steadied the hammock with the bristles. The swaying stopped.

"Must have just been the wind," said Sky, now full of bravado. "You lot were crazy to be scared. Look, it's just full of clothes." And he brought the broom down hard— smack—on the hammock.

Jack howled as he fell to the wet floor.

Sky turned white. His bottom lip quivered for a second before he ran screaming from the room.

"Ghost!" yelled the others as they stumbled and fought their way out of the forecastle, slamming the door behind them. In less than a second, the room was clear. Jack heard the bolt fly across the outside of the door.

He pulled himself up onto the empty bench and grabbed the nearest mug. He was extremely thirsty and quickly downed the dregs of the lukewarm liquid, which, he was surprised to find, was tea. Jack drained every mug. When he finished, he sat and stared at the water that slopped across the floor. Dark thoughts crowded his mind.

What had happened to the *Belle?* Had the bomb exploded? Were his father and the crew still alive? Were they stranded on the ice? What about Gadfly? Was he all right? Had the saboteurs stolen the *Viper?*

Jack shook his head and tried to think clearly. If the airship crew were stranded on the ice, they'd be able to radio for help. Rescue parties would be searching for them. They'd be all right, wouldn't they?

As Jack stood, the strap of the sextant case, which was still looped around his body, caught on the edge of the table. Jack stopped. He had the airship's only sextant. The voices had said the airship was locked off course. The airship crew wouldn't know where they were. And if they didn't know where they were, how could they tell the rescue parties where to find them?

Chapter 7

The Thieves

A shadow fell across the patch of sunlight on the fore-castle floor. Jack looked up and saw a man silhouetted against the bright morning sky.

"Come into the light," the man growled at him.

Jack slowly leaned forward.

"He's no ghost!" the man exclaimed. Footsteps crossed the forecastle roof and skittered down the steps of the companionway.

Jack glanced down at the sextant. It would be the first thing the pirates took from him. He couldn't let that happen. Quickly Jack lifted the case over his head and looked for a place to hide it.

At the rear of the forecastle, Jack spotted a chest. He darted over and opened it. It was full of dirty clothes, but at least they were dry. Jack wrapped a ratty sweater around the sextant, then stashed the bundle at the bottom of the chest.

When this was done, he sprang toward the table, reaching it just as the bolt was drawn back. A second later the door flew open and crashed against the wall with an almighty bang.

"Come out here! Come on. Out here now!"

Jack peered through the door. The man now stood on the deck with a pistol in his hand. He was obviously the captain; Quixote, the men had called him. He seemed to swallow up most of the space on the deck, though in truth, he was not that much broader or taller than the other men. The crew were gathered in a clump behind him, muttering amongst themselves. Jack heard the whispered words "ghosts," "bad luck," and "Jonah."

"Quiet," snapped Quixote, jerking around. As he did so, the light fell across his face.

Jack gasped. It wasn't the hardness of the captain's features that frightened him, or the windburned skin on the gaunt cheeks; nor was it the wild hair as black as a bull's back, or the thick scowling brows, or the white teeth that flashed when he spoke to his men. It was the piercing look in the captain's eyes that terrified Jack. It was as cold and as deep and as cruel as the sea.

Jack backed into the shadows and knocked against

the table, sending a plate crashing to the floor. The captain swiftly turned and, brandishing the pistol, took a step toward the forecastle.

"Come out now or I start shooting for sport," he warned.

Jack didn't doubt that he would. Lifting his hands above his head, Jack stepped, blinking, into the light.

"By the head of Gregor Ladislav Lavinovich," declared the captain. "This lad's pale and pasty, but he's no ghost. See how he shakes at the sight of my gun, and that's blood on his head."

Captain Quixote stuck his pistol back in his belt and, grabbing Jack by the chin, examined the cut on his head. Jack blinked up at him. The cold light he had seen in the captain's eyes was gone. His eyes were bright now and sparkled like the sun on the sea.

"It's just a scrape," said Quixote, letting go of Jack's chin. "It'll clean up all right."

Jack opened and closed his mouth, working his jaw to get some feeling back.

"Search him!" commanded the captain, and the two men with eye patches tentatively stepped forward. Jack could see now that they were identical twins. Everything about them was the same except for their eye patches. One man's covered his left eye, the other man's his right.

Neither of them spoke as they searched Jack. One pulled Jack's greatcoat from his shoulders and rifled through the pockets while the other patted him down.

"Nothing, Captain," said the one with the eye patch over his right eye. He let Jack's coat fall to the deck.

"Thank you, Thomas," said the captain. The man returned to his place in line.

"He's nothing in his pockets, but I'll wager he's bad luck," said the other. "He probably fell off the *N—*" The man with the patch on his left eye stopped. The other men gasped and shrank back.

"What was that?" growled the captain.

"I—er—only meant . . . he's a Jonah. He'll bring doom and disaster to the ship. We should throw him back."

"You're a fool, Horatio Fell," snarled Quixote. "As big a fool as your brother. You're all Jonahs. I picked you all up out of the sea, for better or for worse. Do you think that I should throw you all back? I'm not going to waste an extra pair of hands. Sky?"

"Aye, Captain?"

"Take this boy to the galley. Cook'll put him to work. You can fetch my breakfast while you're there. A man could die of hunger on this ship. And *no sugar!*"

"Not even a—"

"None!" the captain's eyes glittered menacingly.

"Aye, captain," Sky answered. He took Jack by the shoulder and, pushing him through the circle of grim-faced men, led him belowdecks.

They found the cook sleeping in the galley, sprawled on his back beneath the stove. A flagon rolled next to him and rivulets of syrup dribbled down his fat chin. He half opened one eye; it was bloodshot and swam blearily in its socket. Recognizing neither Jack nor Sky, he gave up, snorted, and went back to sleep.

"That's Treacle, the cook," stammered Sky. "Do you know how to make breakfast?"

"Um . . . ," Jack began.

"Well, you'd better start learning!" Sky snapped, screwing his face into an angry scowl. Suddenly the scowl fell away and his voice dropped to a whisper. "Listen, you're the youngest on this ship now and that means I'm supposed to tell you what to do. If you don't do what I say, the others'll laugh at me and my life won't be worth living. So please, make the captain's breakfast. Please." At the sound of footsteps Sky snapped, "You . . . you . . . you'd better look sharp." Then he pushed Jack into the galley and hurried away.

Jack peered into the tiny galley. It was filthy and cramped. Most of the space was taken by the huge iron stove, which stood on four claw-shaped legs. The stove was disgusting. The top was smeared with blackened grease that had solidified into rancid dribbles along the edges. The hard black bubbles shone like polished jet. Two dismal, damp gray rags hung in tatters along the rail at the front.

Next to the stove, a troughlike sink was piled high with dirty dishes. The walls were splashed with old food, and the tiles on the floor were black with grime. A sickly sweet smell hung in the air.

Jack felt queasy. How was he going to make the captain's breakfast? Perhaps he ought to try and rouse the cook. He nudged the sleeping man with his foot, but the cook just continued snoring.

Jack sank to the floor and pressed his forehead against his knees. What had happened to the men on the *Belle?* What had happened to his father and Gadfly? Jack groaned. He shouldn't have broken his promise to his father. He shouldn't have climbed the air shaft. And the sextant! Jack groaned again. He had their only sextant. Without it they had no way of knowing where they were. No way at all. Jack hung his head and listened to the creaking ship. He had to do something. But what? The ship creaked as it rose against a wave.

Of course, the ship! The *Hyperion* would be big enough to rescue the crew of the *Belle*. He had the airship's last reading; from that, the ship's navigator could work out exact coordinates and find the *Belle*. All he needed to do was persuade Captain Quixote to help him; to do that, Jack needed to get on Captain Quixote's good side. Jack quickly stood and began to gather the things needed to make the captain's breakfast.

Beneath the stove the cook shifted in his sleep, and a

small gray cat peered out from behind him. Its fur was matted and greasy, and its tail was ragged at the end. It meowed pitifully and strained against its string leash, nearly strangling itself every time it moved.

Jack couldn't bear to see it all tangled up. He took a carving knife from the sink and deftly cut the string.

"There you go," he said. Without a backward glance, the cat leaped over the cook and scampered out of the galley.

Jack lit the stove, set a pan on the flame, and threw in three fat slices of bacon. The heat from the stove and the smell of the food soon woke the cook, who scratched his armpit and smacked his lips.

"Lard! Lard . . . Here Lardy-kins . . . ," he called blearily. He reached out with his hand; his fingers, swollen and shiny like unpricked sausages, fumbled across the filthy floor. They groped around the foot of the stove, found the cut string, and stopped. The cook sat up quickly and banged his head against the underside of the stove.

"*Lard!*" he called. "*Lard!* Lardy-kins—here, kitty-kitty." He made kissing noises with his chubby lips and called again and again until it became clear that Lard wasn't going to answer.

"Drat and blast it!" he cursed as he pulled himself out from beneath the stove. "And who the blazes are you?" he asked when he saw Jack. Jack didn't know what to say. The cook eyed him wearily. "Are you going to tell me or shall I just go blue in the face trying to guess?"

"My name's Jack," replied Jack. "Jack Black."

"Is it now?" said the cook as he raised his flagon of sticky syrup to his lips, all the while keeping his blood-shot eyes on Jack.

When he'd taken a slug at the flagon, he leaned in close to Jack and hissed, "Did you set my cat free?" His breath was warm and sugary, and his teeth were as rotten as long-dead tree trunks.

"His string was choking him. He was in pain," stammered Jack.

"Ha! He used that trick, did he?" said the cook, taking another long draft of syrup. When he finished, he wiped his glistening chin with the back of his wrist. "Well, lad, I don't blame you for falling for his little trick. I bet he was meowing like a poor lost kitten. But there'll be hell to pay when Quixote finds out that my Lard's running about free as air. You see, Lard loves the captain, but the captain can't stand Lard. The cat makes him sneeze something terrible. Now I'll be the one who lands in the soup for letting Lard free. Well, I'll just tell him you did it. That's what I'll do. Pass me another flagon of syrup, this one's finished." The cook waggled a fat finger at the flagons that were stacked in the corner.

Jack passed him one. The cook nodded his thanks, then pulled the cork out and put the flagon to his lips.

"Treacle's my name!" he said as he lowered the flagon and wiped his sweaty forehead on his shoulder. "I love my little Lard," he added in a tearful whisper.

Jack carefully cracked three eggs into the pan. The edges of the eggs bubbled and shot scalding fat across the back of his hand. The cook watched him.

"When was the last time you saw land?" he asked.

Jack stopped. Now that he thought about it, he wasn't sure. "How long were we in that storm?" he asked in reply.

Mr. Treacle counted the days on his fat, sticky fingers.

"One, two, er . . . three, I believe," he said finally. "Yes, three!"

"Three days?" gasped Jack. "I was asleep for three days? That means it's almost a week since the launch of the *Belle*." Jack shook his head. It seemed much longer somehow. A whole lifetime ago, perhaps.

The cook sighed. "Were the boughs heavy with blossom when you left home?" he asked wistfully.

"They were just coming into bloom," said Jack as he poked the knife under an egg to lift it from the pan.

The cook smiled.

"I haven't seen the blossom in seventeen years," he said, wiping his mouth. "You get to miss things like that. You'll find out soon enough."

"I'll be back home before the blossom's gone," Jack said.

The cook shook his head. "Oh, dear, has no one told you yet?"

Jack narrowed his eyes. "Told me what?"

"You're part of the crew now, lad," Treacle said. "You'll never get away from here. Not till you die."

The eggs and bacon sizzled in the pan, but Jack had forgotten about them. "I don't believe that," he murmured.

"We haven't put into a port in twenty-odd years," said the cook. "There's some that say the ship is a miracle ship, that we should by rights all be drowned at the bottom of the sea. The number of times we've come close to losing her can't be counted, not on your fingers and mine put together. But there are others that say she's cursed, that she cannot put into port. Whenever we get close to land, I mean real land with towns and villages and people, mysterious winds blow up and steer us far off course. Every man on this ship was brought here by luck, good or bad, and all of us have stayed. You're part of this crew now, lad, and you'd better learn to like it. You're going to be here for a very long time."

"That can't be true," Jack whispered.

"You just ask anyone," replied the cook, tipping the flagon to his lips.

"Hurry it up down there," hollered Sky from above. "Captain wants his breakfast."

Jack quickly lifted the eggs and bacon onto the plate.

"Hey, you forgot to sweeten his eggs," cried the cook. And Jack only just managed to get by before he could douse the captain's breakfast in syrup.

Chapter 8

Captain Quixote

Jack peered through a crack in the door of Quixote's cabin. He could see the captain hunched over his desk studying a map and occasionally making a note in a small book. Jack pulled his face away and looked out to sea. Somewhere to the north lay the Polar Sea and somewhere beyond that his father and the crew of the *Belle*. He had to do something to help them.

Jack knocked on the door with his free hand. There was a pause, then Quixote bellowed, "Come in!"

Jack entered with the plate of food and set it on the desk. He noticed that the notebook the captain had been writing in had disappeared.

The captain eyed his food warily. "Any sugar on it?" he asked.

Jack shook his head.

"Good! Very good," said Quixote, rubbing his hands together. His eyes twinkled, and he nodded at Jack. "You can tell me your story while I eat," he said. He grabbed his knife and fork, cut through a slice of bacon, and popped it in his mouth. He closed his eyes and sighed as he chewed.

Jack took a deep breath. "You've got to turn your ship around," he said. "It's a matter of life and death! You see, my father and his crew . . . They'll all be on the ice by now. . . . The bomb on the airship will have exploded and they'll be stranded and I'm the only one who knows where they are! We've got to get to them, we've got to . . ."

Quixote slammed his hand down so hard on the desk that the plate leaped.

"Hold on!" he said through a mouthful of bacon. He took a slurp of tea and swallowed to clear his mouth. "First things first," he said, spearing another piece of bacon and pushing runny egg on top of it. "First, I want to know how you got on board my ship."

Jack quickly told him everything that had happened. He told him about the *Bellerophon*, and the launch, and Gadfly's plane, and Bill Fallow's cut on his hand. He told him about how he'd climbed the air shaft and taken the reading, and how he'd heard the voices saying there was a bomb planted on the tail.

"You see," he said urgently, "the airship was off

course, and I'm the only one who knows where it was headed when it crashed. We must go and find them. No one else will be able to."

"Ha!" Quixote said as he pushed away the empty plate and wiped the corners of his mouth with his thumb and finger. "That's quite a story. Ships that fly, eh? Airships? Ha! It's a good tale," he added, turning around. "I suppose you don't want to tell me the truth, but it doesn't matter. Everyone on this ship has something they'd rather hide."

"But it's *true*," Jack insisted. "You must believe me!"

"How can I?" asked Quixote. "You talk of flying machines, of 'air' ships, but I've never seen one. You say you fell thousands of feet, but how would you still be alive if you had?"

Jack shook his head. "My father . . . the crew . . . they're stranded. They need rescuing. You have to take me back to the Polar Sea!"

Quixote looked up sharply. "The Polar Sea?" His face turned ashen, and his voice grew cold. "No."

"Then take me to the nearest port," Jack pleaded.

"No!" The captain stood and stared out at the endless sea.

"Why not?" asked Jack.

The captain turned swiftly. His eyes were burning like ice. "By the head of Gregor Ladislav Lavinovich," he hissed, "this ship won't put into port until . . ." Quixote stopped and ran his hands over his face. "No," he said, "I cannot fulfill that promise, but neither can I break it. This ship hasn't put into port for over twenty-five years, and now she never will."

Quixote sank into his chair and looked up at Jack. "Wherever you came from, this ship saved your life. Now you belong to her. You might as well accept it like the others did. The sea is your home now."

Quixote pulled out the map again and began to study it. His down-turned face was as dark as thunder. The interview was over.

A moment later Jack stood outside Quixote's cabin, shivering in the wind. He looked for his greatcoat and saw with surprise that it had been hung neatly from a belaying pin along the rail. Jack took it down and put it on, hitching the collar up around his ears to shield them from the wind.

Jack stared over the rail at the thin dark line of the northern horizon. Somewhere out there his father and the crew of the *Belle* were stranded, and he could do nothing to help them. Maybe if he could convince Quixote that his story was true, maybe then he'd take Jack back to the Polar Sea.

Suddenly Quixote's cabin door burst open and the captain came flying out. His eyes were red and fiery and he was sneezing great bone-rattling sneezes. He grabbed Jack's arm.

"Find . . . that . . . cat," he said breathlessly, pointing back into his cabin.

Jack hunted beneath the desk and pushed aside a pile of maps. Lard ran out and made straight for the captain. He would have gotten there, too, if Jack hadn't leaped after him and grabbed him around the middle.

It was as Jack got to his feet that he noticed all the maps he'd knocked over. Holding the cat in one hand, he began to rifle through them with the other.

Perhaps, he thought, *there's a chart that would show me how to get to the Polar Sea.*

"There's no use looking at them," wheezed Quixote. "They won't be of any use. You won't be leaving this ship. D'you hear me? Now take the cat and get out!" Quixote was still sneezing. "And you can tell the cook the next time I find that animal loose on my ship, I'll throw it overboard and him with it."

I bet you would, thought Jack. He dropped the maps on the floor and left.

Chapter 9

The Engineer

The wind picked up, and the ship skimmed across the waves. They sailed south, heading farther and farther away from Jack's father.

Jack leaned against the rail and stared down at the racing blue-green water. *If only I could radio for help*, he thought. Jack gripped the rail. Radio! That was it! If there was a radio on board, he could send the reading he had taken on the airship to the rescue parties. Jack hurried to get the sextant.

The windowless forecastle was dark and quiet. No lantern was lit, and someone had strung a piece of sailcloth across the hole in the ceiling. Although it was still daylight three of the crew were asleep in their hammocks. The air in the forecastle was thick with their sleepy breath. One of the sleepers groaned but didn't wake.

Jack cautiously wended his way between the swaying hammocks until he reached the chest at the far end of the forecastle.

Silently he dug through the clothes and found the bundle at the bottom. He was relieved to find the sextant still there. Jack pulled it out and unfastened the buckle on the strap. Quickly he slipped the strap under his coat and around his neck, refastened the buckle, and then buttoned his coat to hide the sextant from prying eyes. He was halfway to the door when someone in the room began to sing.

My love is like a red, red rose
That's newly sprung in June.

Jack stood stock-still and stared at the singer. It was one of the twins. His eye patch covered his right eye. *Thomas*, thought Jack. Thomas was sprawled across a musty hammock with his legs hanging down, one on either side. His left eye was closed in sleep, but his mouth was smiling like a baby's. He had a beautiful voice:

My love is like a melody
That's sweetly sung in tune.

Then Thomas stopped singing and another voice

took over. Jack wheeled around and saw Horatio lying in the far hammock. He was singing now.

> *As fair art thou, my bonnie lass,*
> *So deep in love am I.*
> *And I will love thee still, my dear,*
> *Till a' the seas gang dry.*

Then both twins began to sing together, and the harmony was sublime.

> *Till a' the seas gang dry, my dear,*
> *And the rocks melt wi' the sun.*
> *And I will love thee still, my dear,*
> *While the sands o' life shall run.*

"'Ere, what are you gawking at?"

Jack leaped back. Thomas was staring at him with his good eye.

"The song . . . ," Jack said. "Your singing . . . I was listening . . ."

"Eh? What are you talking about?" growled Horatio. "Go on, get out of here! Let a man get some sleep. Singing? Catch me singing. Get out of it or I'll give you what for!" And he shook a gnarled fist the size of a boy's head in Jack's face.

Jack didn't wait to be told twice. He bolted out of the

forecastle more determined than ever to find the ship's radio. It didn't take him long to search the deck. In the rigging, Eric Lamb, Sky, and Simon were taking in the sails. Jack skirted around the edge of the deck to avoid attracting their attention. When he was certain that there was no radio on the upper decks, he found the main hatch and went below.

As he went down the steps, Jack heard the ship's engines come on, thrumming steadily. But somewhere beneath the noise Jack thought he could hear the distinctive pattern of a Morse code signal. Jack's heart leaped. A Morse signal meant only one thing—a radio. Jack stumbled through a dark passageway toward the sound, pressing on until he came to the engine room. Pausing by the door, he could hear the signal inside.

Strange, he thought, *to have the radio so close to the engine. It must be hard to hear messages.*

The engine room looked nothing like the rest of the ship. Filled with a complex but neat maze of copper and brass pipes, pistons, and pumps, it was an island of order in a sea of disarray. Against the steady, regular beat of the engine came the irregular and insistent Morse signal.

Jack edged his way past the moving mass of pistons and cylinders. In the far corner of the room, pressed up against the wall, was a small wooden desk. Before it sat a man. He had his back to Jack. On one corner of the desk stood a tin bucket, collecting water that fell through a hole in the ceiling. *Ping, ping, plink. Ping, ping, plink,* the water sang as it landed in the bucket. Jack's heart fell. There was his radio; there was his Morse signal.

Jack inched forward until he was able to peer over the man's shoulder. Laid out across the desk was a large blueprint of a warship. In one corner of the plan, the word NEMESIS was engraved in large curly letters above a complicated crest. It was the ship Jack had seen as he'd fallen! Jack stared at the huge funnels and the massive engines until the little man, sensing that he was not alone, carefully folded up the drawing and slipped it into an envelope. Then, removing his spectacles, he turned and looked at Jack.

"Do you have a name?" he asked.

"Jack," replied Jack.

"A good name for an adventurer," said the man. He pulled a handkerchief from his waistcoat pocket and began cleaning the lenses of his spectacles. "I no longer have a name. I lost it when I came on board. I'm just called the engineer. Now tell me your story, and try not to leave anything out. The details are often important."

Jack told him his story from beginning to end. When he had finished, the engineer sat back in his chair.

"Incredible," he said. "Unbelievable! This ship is indeed a miracle ship. Do you know the chances of surviving a fall like that? A million, no, ten million to one. At least!"

"You mean you believe me?" Jack asked.

"Of course I do," said the engineer.

"The captain doesn't," Jack said. "He won't help me. He says I have to stay here forever, but I can't. I have to help my father. I need to . . . I thought I could radio for help."

"That is an excellent idea," said the engineer, "but I'm afraid we don't have a radi—"

A shrill, piercing whistle interrupted him.

"That is the call for all hands on deck," the engineer said. He jabbed his thumb skyward. "You had better go. They will expect you up there."

Jack hesitated. "Do you think you could persuade the captain to go back to the Polar Sea and help me find my father?" he asked.

"No, I do not think I can," answered the engineer with a sad shake of his head. "That is probably the last thing I can persuade him to do." The whistle sounded a second time. The engineer smiled and replaced his glasses on his nose. "You had better hurry," he said. "You don't want to be late."

Chapter 10

A Challenge for Quixote

As Jack watched the crew assemble on deck, he was surprised to find that they didn't look half as menacing as they had earlier. Now they were all smiling cheerily. Even the twins, with their swarthy chins and grim eye patches, had twinkles in their good eyes. Mr. Treacle, the cook, lay fast asleep beneath the companionway, his vast body striped with the shadows of the steps. Only the engineer was missing.

Quixote stood above them on the poop deck and brandished a red bandanna.

"What a bright and beautiful day it is," he declared, his smile broadening by the moment. "I think it's time for a game of challenges!"

The crew cheered.

"Who dares to challenge me?" bellowed the captain.

"And what does he dare me to do?"

The crew all shouted at once.

"Wait! Wait!" cried the captain, holding up his hand. "One at a time. Come on, who has a fair challenge for their captain?"

"Run all the way around the ship on the rail," cried one of the twins.

"Cross the stays and back!" said the other.

"Backward!"

"Blindfolded!"

The captain held up his hands, and the men fell silent. "Tom Fell, do you agree with your brother?"

Both twins grunted and turned their backs on each other. The captain laughed. "What about the rest of you? Do you dare me to run backward around the rail with my eyes bound? I'm not afraid. Quixote has never been known to refuse a dare. Now who's for a wager? Who'll put their money where their captain's life is?" He threw his cap onto the deck.

The men made their bets. They used large rough pebbles for money.

One of the twins, Thomas Fell, threw down two stones that clanked together as they tumbled into the upturned hat. "I bet two rubies that we have to fish you out before you get halfway around," he said. "Looks like you'd have some company if you fell in," he added, peering over the rail.

The men rushed to the rail and saw the shadow of a great shark beside the ship.

"Let's change the challenge," urged Horatio, growing nervous.

"Change it? Never!" laughed Quixote. "Gentlemen, bets have been made. Quixote's not the man to back down."

The hat was overflowing with the dull stones. Quixote snatched one up and laughed.

"My! What a lack of faith my shipmates show," he said. "If I win, all these precious darlings'll be mine."

"Why does he call them precious?" Jack asked Sky.

"Because that's what they are. Look, these are sapphires." Sky pulled two pebbles from his pocket and scratched one against the other. The scratch in the stone gleamed. Jack gasped.

"If all those pebbles are uncut gemstones," he said, "there must be a fortune in that hat." He reached out to touch the sapphire, but Sky snatched it away.

"Oh, no, you don't," he stammered. "Get your own."

"Has everybody made their bets?" asked Quixote.

"Aye!" answered the crew.

"Then let's go. Here, boy, bind my eyes!" He thrust the red bandanna toward Jack. Jack tied it across Quixote's eyes.

"Good!" said Quixote. "Now, spin me around three times and point me to starboard."

When Jack let go, the captain staggered to the rail with his hands outstretched like a drunkard on a moonless night. Then with one agile leap he jumped up on the narrow rail. Almost immediately, the sea, which had been calm, began to swell.

The captain held out his arms to steady himself, then set off at a trot backward toward the stern. He was extremely surefooted. He didn't even slow down as he skipped and ducked and weaved past the main shrouds.

As he approached the poop deck, he reached blindly for a rope and, finding one, hoisted himself up onto the higher rail. He landed on his toes and set off again, skipping backward past the mizzen shrouds as easily as most men run forward. He trotted around the stern and hopped over each of the timber heads that protruded above the rail. When he came to the small skiff, hanging on davits along the port side, he turned sideways. There was just enough room to squeeze by.

As Quixote passed the little boat, Jack suddenly had an idea. What if he stole the skiff and escaped? He couldn't sail north to rescue his father, but perhaps he could reach land and get in touch with the rescue parties. He felt a surge of excitement. All he needed was a compass and a chart and he could be on his way.

He glanced around. Quixote's cabin door was close by. There would be a compass in there and perhaps a map he could use as well. Quietly he slipped away from the rest of the crew.

In Quixote's cabin, he knelt on the floor and quickly rifled through the captain's maps. He found three that might serve him. As he stood up, he noticed a strange little glass bottle on one of the shelves. It had a brown paper map furled inside. Jack picked it up and was about to open it when he heard the men outside groan.

Peeking through the door, Jack saw Quixote stumbling on the rail. The captain lunged forward with a superhuman effort and grabbed on to the ratlines. The crew cheered as Quixote set off running again.

Jack didn't have much time. He set the bottle back on the shelf and opened the drawers in the desk, searching for a compass. He soon found a small one made of silver. As he picked it up, he noticed a journal lying beside it in the drawer. It was open, and its pages were covered with large childish writing. Jack tried to read it, but it didn't make any sense. The letters were all misshapen or backward. As he turned the pages, the writing gave way to crude drawings of warships with their guns ablaze.

A cheer outside warned Jack that the captain had almost finished his challenge. He quickly put the journal back in the drawer, stuffed the compass in his pocket and the maps inside his shirt, and slipped out of the captain's cabin. Taking his place by Sky, he sneaked a look at the skiff and smiled to himself.

Quixote had circled the ship and returned to the point on the rail where he had begun his challenge. He paused for a moment, then threw himself into a high somersault. Up and over he went, twisting his body in the air. He landed neatly on his toes, yanked the blindfold from his eyes, and laughed as he picked up the hat full of stones.

"I believe these are mine!" he cried, then he pointed to Jack. "Fetch me some water, lad. Hurry."

The maps inside Jack's shirt prickled against his chest as he bent over the rim of the water barrel and scooped stale water from the bottom. Quixote drank greedily, then peered in the water barrel to check the contents.

"We'll have to get in more supplies, lads," he said. "We're down on food as well. We'll go for the first ship we see in the morning. I want everyone to keep an eye out."

The crew cheered again. Attacking ships was obviously something they enjoyed. Jack felt sick and disgusted. These men were nothing more than a bunch of dirty thieves.

He turned away from them and gazed out to sea. As he stared across the gray waters, he saw the distant silhouette of a large bird flying north.

A small puff of smoke, black against the white clouds, made Jack's heart leap for joy. It wasn't a bird—it was a plane!

"Look! Look!" he cried. "A plane! An airplane! There to the north. See? I was telling the truth. Come on, we have to signal to her." He waved his arms high above his head.

Quixote peered up into the sky and laughed. He saw nothing more than a dark speck against the sky. "This boy says that men have invented machines that can fly," the captain said. "What do you think of that?"

The crew laughed along with their captain.

Jack spun around and glared angrily at Quixote, which made the crew laugh all the more. He turned from them and stared down at the steely waters. If he was going to escape in the skiff he'd need supplies. He would sneak into the hold when the others were having their supper. Then he could leave tonight. *The sooner I'm off this rotten ship,* Jack thought, *the better.*

In the Hold

The light from Jack's lantern swayed up and down the creaking walls as he descended into the dark hold.

Like the water barrel, the hold was almost empty. There were two small casks of water, a tiny wooden tub of butter, a box of stale ship biscuits, and a barrel less than a quarter full of wormy, rank-smelling apples. There were also a few sacks of sugar and some of flour.

Jack spread one of the greasy towels he'd taken from the galley, picked out ten of the least wormy apples, and laid them on the cloth. He found a few broken biscuits and carefully put them beside the apples. Then he tied the four corners of the cloth together and put it and one of the small casks of water behind the ladder. He would come back and get it later when everyone was asleep.

He was about to leave when he heard footsteps above

him. Someone was coming through the hatch! Jack blew out his lamp and hid beneath the ladder just as a fat foot stepped onto the top rung.

Holding a lantern in one hand, a flagon of syrup in the other, and with Lard balancing on his shoulder, Mr. Treacle half fell down the ladder.

Jack held his breath as the cook set down the lantern, grabbed a sack of sugar by the ears, and hoisted it onto his shoulder. Lard quickly skittered to the far end of the opposite shoulder. Then, picking up the lamp, Mr. Treacle tottered back along the aisle. It was as he was climbing back up the ladder that he stumbled and his knife fell from his belt. It slipped between the rungs, skimmed past Jack's ear, and sank its point deep into the floorboards.

Mr. Treacle crouched down and jabbed his hand between the rungs, searching for the knife.

Jack didn't want the cook to find him there, so he silently pulled the knife out of the boards and held the handle out. Mr. Treacle's fingers closed around it. Then he put it back in his belt and struggled up the rest of the ladder. It took three attempts, but finally he was gone.

Jack waited, crouched in the shadows, until he could hear the cook banging about in the galley. It wasn't until the air turned sweet with the smell of boiling sugar that he stole back up the ladder.

Once on deck, Jack turned his face to the wind,

opened his mouth, and sucked in the fresh clean air. The sun was low in the sky. Soon it would be properly dark, and Jack would make his escape.

The moon rose early and was in the sky long before the sun had set. But in the growing darkness, heavy clouds gathered and hid the moon from sight. This was just what Jack wanted. A nice dark night.

When Mr. Treacle hollered for Jack, he hurried down to the galley, where the cook thrust a pot of watery stew into his hands.

"Carry this up to the forecastle," he said. "And if they say it's not enough, tell them they can put some syrup in it. When you've done that, you can come back here and clean up. I'm going to have a nice, peaceful nap."

Suddenly Jack realized how hungry he was. He hadn't eaten since he'd arrived on the *Hyperion*. The stew looked revolting and smelled even worse, but he would happily have eaten some if he'd had the chance. He only wanted a small bowlful, but as soon as he set it down on the table the men pounced on the pot like tigers and within seconds it was empty.

Jack carried the empty pot and dirty plates back to the galley and dumped them in the sink. There was no sign of Treacle, and Jack didn't feel like washing the dishes. He would be long gone before anyone thought to bother him about it. Instead, he hurried to the hold and waited in the darkness until the ship fell quiet. When he was sure the crew were asleep, he picked up his bundle and crept up the stairs and out onto the deck. He could hear men snoring behind the forecastle door as he sneaked across the deck to the skiff.

When he reached the little boat, he put the bundle of food and the water cask into it, then hoisted himself up. He was about to climb in when something small and furry leaped out at him. It was Treacle's cat. Jack peered over the edge of the skiff, and his heart sank.

The cook was sound asleep in the bottom of the skiff. As Jack watched, Mr. Treacle shifted and, trying to make himself more comfortable, groggily pushed Jack's supplies overboard. Jack listened in horror as they landed in the sea with a loud *splash*. Jack groaned, sank against the rail, and buried his head on his knees.

Chapter 12

The Robbery

"Come on, wake up," commanded Eric Lamb, shaking Jack roughly by the shoulder. "Captain's been asking for you."

Jack jerked awake, not knowing for a moment where he was. The sun was up, and he was slumped against the rail next to the skiff. He must have fallen asleep! Someone had covered him with a blanket in the night. Jack threw it off and got to his feet.

To his amazement the *Hyperion* was now alongside a big four-masted ship. LADY ANNE was painted in gold along her prow. The crew of the *Hyperion* were carrying boxes and crates across a narrow plank that had been laid between the two ships. As they stacked them on the *Hyperion*'s deck, it dawned on Jack that he was witnessing a robbery.

Eric Lamb grabbed his arm and dragged him to the plank. "Get over there and get to work," he said, pushing him along. Jack, not wanting to fall into the sea, hurried across.

Quixote stood over the crew of the *Lady Anne*, who were tied to the mainmast. Jack was surprised to see that they didn't seem concerned that they were being robbed by pirates. They were joking and laughing with Quixote.

"Pitch in there, lad," Quixote shouted when he saw Jack. "I'll not have wastrels on my ship."

"I'm not a thief," Jack said boldly. "I'm not going to steal for you."

Quixote strode over to him. "So you're not a thief, eh? Well, I'd like to know what you'd call the person who took my compass and my maps. If that's not theft, what is it?"

Jack shut his mouth. He hadn't thought that he was stealing anything. Quixote had so many maps. He was only borrowing. No, he wasn't. Even though he was doing it to help his father, Jack had still stolen the compass and the maps. Quixote was right.

Jack pulled the compass out of his pocket and the maps from the front of his shirt. Quixote took them.

"Horatio, put this lad to work," he growled.

The hold of the *Lady Anne* was a treasure trove of food. There were smoked hams and cheeses, and strings of onions, garlic, and dried peppers swung from the beams. Huge salamis wrapped in waxed paper and sealed with gold labels were strapped together and hung like bunches of bananas along the wall. There were boxes of dried fruit, barrels of fresh green apples, crates of potatoes, and baskets of rice. Sacks of flour, sugar, and oats were stacked high on one side. There were tins of salmon and sardines and rice pudding, and even bigger tins of marmalade and jam. Jack stared up at them and felt his mouth fill with water. Horatio nudged his arm.

"Here, you'll need some of this if you're going to be any use," he said, and handed Jack a hunk of bread and cheese. Jack grabbed it and began to eat so fast that Horatio burst out laughing.

"Steady, lad," he said. "You've got to chew or you'll choke to death. I guess you were pretty hungry, eh?"

Jack nodded and closed his eyes as he chewed. Nothing had ever tasted so good to him.

"When you've finished with that, carry something up, will you, there's a good lad." Horatio patted him on the head and then picked up a nearby crate and lifted it onto his shoulder.

Jack ate the rest of his bread. When he'd finished, he made his way between the spice jars and the sausages until he found what he thought Quixote wanted. In the middle of the hold was a small chest full of gold ingots. Jack struggled to lift the chest, but it was far too heavy for him. He would have to take it piece by piece. He opened the lid and lifted out a solid gold bar. It was so heavy that it took him a few minutes to carry it to the deck.

"Oh, no, take that back!" groaned Quixote when he saw Jack staggering up with the gold. "That's no good to us. We'll get these fellows in trouble if we take that. Bring useful things—food, cigars, sewing needles, that sort of thing. They don't mind sharing that with us."

Bewildered, Jack returned the gold to where he'd found it and closed the chest.

For the next few hours he worked harder than he'd ever worked in his entire life. He carried sack after sack of potatoes, flour, and dried peas, and put them where he was told to put them on the deck of the *Lady Anne*. He lost count of how many times he went up and down the steps, and he lost count of how many things he brought up from the hold. It was long after midday when he heard Quixote shout, "That's enough for now, lads. Go on back to the ship."

The crew of the *Hyperion* hurried across the plank.

"You haven't finished yet," he said to Jack. "Come with me."

Quixote led him past the crew of the *Lady Anne*.

"I just want to see what books you've got, Captain," said Quixote.

"The ones I haven't read are on the top shelf," said the captain of the *Lady Anne*. "Leave those, if you would."

"Of course," called Quixote with a gallantry that surprised Jack.

The captain's cabin was a pleasant wood-paneled room with two low book cabinets on either side of the door. Quixote opened one of them and began to pull books from the shelves.

"Aha," he said as he peered at the title of one. "We'll take this." He handed it to Jack and took another book.

"Oho, this one's a good read," Quixote laughed.

Jack looked at the book. It was called *Higher Mathematics*. It didn't sound like a good read.

"Ah," Quixote nodded sagely at another book, but this time Jack noticed that he was reading the title upside down. The captain added the book to the growing pile in Jack's arms, then returned to the cabinet. He pulled out book after book and soon the pile was as high as Jack's head and his arms felt close to breaking.

"Hmmm. That'll do," said Quixote at last. "Let's get going."

As they were leaving the cabin, Quixote caught sight of a beautiful silk dress hanging on the back of the door. The dress was a rich, deep blue and shone like a sapphire.

"Humph," he said. "It's probably meant for the captain's wife, but I know someone who needs it more." And with that he slung the dress over his shoulder.

"Oh, I say, man," cried the captain when he saw Quixote. "It's all very well taking my books; indeed, you're welcome to them. But that dress is a special present for my wife. Have a heart, won't you?"

Quixote smiled at the captain. "Perhaps these will make a better present for your wife." He reached into his pocket, brought out two of the stones he had won in the game of challenges, and handed them to the captain.

The captain held them to his eye. "Sapphires!" he gasped. "Are they real? Are they stolen?"

"They're real, but they're not stolen. Unless you call taking from the earth stealing. And if you do, we're all of us thieves." Quixote turned to the captive crew and smiled. "Gentlemen, for the goods which you have so kindly . . . er . . . donated, a small token of our appreciation." He dug deep into another pocket and brought out a handful of rough gemstones. "I think these should cover your losses." He put the stones on the deck, and the crew beamed with pleasure.

Staggering beneath the books, Jack edged out onto the rough plank between the ships. It rocked underfoot. Jack bit his lip and tried to keep his attention on the towering stack of books and not think about the dark swirling waters below. The crew of the *Hyperion* laughed.

"Come on now, that's it," they said as Jack neared the end of the plank. "Just a little farther, you're almost there. Now, there's a big step up and then you're safe."

Jack couldn't see over the books; he couldn't see that there was no step in front of him. As he gingerly pawed the air with his foot, it was more than the crew could do to stop themselves from laughing out loud. Jack trod down hard on thin air and tumbled to the deck.

"Mind those books, you blockhead," yelled Quixote as he ran across the plank. His eyes burned bright. "I'll lock you in the chicken coop if any of them are damaged. Now pick them up and bring them to my cabin. Hurry. The rest of you, we've got what we wanted, now let's get out of here." And with that he gave a tug on the rope that bound the crew of the *Lady Anne* together. The knots unraveled themselves and the rope fell away, releasing the men.

As the *Hyperion* pulled away from the side of the *Lady Anne,* Jack gazed up and suddenly noticed the radio mast on her poop deck.

"Wait!" he shouted to Eric Lamb at the wheel. Jack ran to the stern. "Let me get back on board!" he cried, but it was too late. The gap between the two ships was already too wide to cross. Jack slammed his fists on the rail. He'd been so wrapped up in carrying boxes and books that he hadn't even thought to look for a radio, or even to ask if they had one. Jack groaned as the *Hyperion* sped across the waters, leaving the *Lady Anne* far behind.

Chapter 13

The Tale of the Fish Boy

Jack was miserable as he helped the cook prepare dinner for the crew. He peeled fresh potatoes and carrots and parsnips while the cook fried onions in butter and cut thick slices of ham. Soon the whole ship was filled with delicious smells, and everybody's mouth was watering. The cook was about to add his customary ladleful of syrup to the stew when Jack, who couldn't bear to see such a fine meal spoiled, stopped his arm and suggested that it might be better if he served the syrup as a side dish. After all, wasn't that the way they did it in the best restaurants? The cook paused with the brimming ladle in midair.

"It would be a way of saving syrup," he said, thinking out loud. "I could always put the leftovers back in the bottle."

Jack agreed that was a fine idea. When the ham stew was bubbling on the stove, all the pots and knives had been washed up, and a small dish had been filled with syrup, Jack took the plates up to the forecastle.

Supper was a great success. It was the finest meal they'd eaten in months. The side dish of syrup had been drained dry by Mr. Treacle, who, seeing that no one was hurrying to add it to their meal, had guzzled it down in one gulp. The foul, fermented confection was having its usual effect on him, and he lolled lazily on the bench.

"Give us a story, Treacle," demanded Eric, slapping the cook hard on the back before he had a chance to doze off.

"'S'not for me to tell other men's stories," he hic-cupped. "You wouldn't catch me dead telling you that someone in this room is really a fish boy." Mr. Treacle's eyes bulged in his sweaty face. The crew exchanged glances and leaned forward to hear more. "Oh, no," said the cook, licking his lips. "You won't hear me telling you how this fish boy, a scaly creature of the deepest deep, changed into a human boy when he was thrown out of the sea by a vengeful father. As fate would have it," Mr. Treacle nodded in deadly earnest, "he fell clean through that roof and into this 'ere forecastle. No sir, you won't catch me telling anybody that."

Then the cook leaned so far forward that he slumped facedown into his syrup bowl and began to snore.

"So, fish boy, is that your story? Is that what happened?" Eric Lamb's eyes twinkled as he spoke. It took Jack a moment to realize the cook had been talking about him.

"That's ridiculous," he said. "I'm no fish boy. I'm a normal boy. I fell off an airship!"

The pirates burst out laughing. Some of them slapped the table, while others slapped their knees.

"What's so funny?" demanded Jack.

Eric wiped a grubby sleeve across his face. "Can't you see?" he said. "What's more ridiculous? A fish boy or an airship? A fish boy is pretty silly, but do you really expect us to believe in ships that fly through the air? I know what the wind feels like at the top of the *Hyperion*'s mainmast. You wouldn't catch me in the rigging of a ship that flew through the air."

Then Thomas leaned forward. "How many sails does your airship have?" he asked.

"How many masts?" asked Horatio.

The questions came quickly, and though they pretended they were in earnest, the pirates were laughing all the time.

"Men have been flying for years," cried Jack in exasperation. But no one was listening to him. Then from far away came an unexpected sound, a humming noise from beyond the clouds. Jack was the first to hear it, and at once, he knew what it was.

He ran out on deck and scanned the sky, then bolted back into the forecastle.

"Hurry," he insisted. "Come and look at this."

The men stopped laughing and hurried on deck.

"Look!" shouted Jack, pointing up into the sky. "Now you'll believe me. Look up there, it's a plane! An airplane!"

The crew shaded their eyes and squinted into the sunset. Silhouetted against pink and purple clouds was a plane. Jack waved frantically as it flew toward the ship. The crew stared up into the sky with their mouths open, each unable to utter a word.

As he came on deck, the engineer asked, "Is it really an airplane?" His spectacles glinted in the last of the sunlight. The crew turned and gaped at him.

"I can't remember the last time he was on deck," muttered Thomas Fell.

"Me neither," said Eric.

Then the plane roared right over the ship and everyone except Jack and the engineer ran for cover. Jack cheered and waved. The plane banked to the right and flew away from the ship, turning in a wide circle.

Quixote came out of his cabin and stood at the rail.

"See," Jack cried when he saw him. "I told you. I told you men could fly."

"Gregor Ladislav Lavinovich!" said Quixote, staring at the plane in amazement. "It really *is* a flying machine.

But it looks as though it won't be flying for long."

Jack shaded his eyes. Small sparking flames were shooting out of the engine and a trail of black smoke suddenly streamed behind the tail fin. The pilot circled above the ship and was obviously going to try to land on the sea. The plane had floats, which would make it easier, but it was going to take a great deal of skill to land safely—the sea was not all that calm. Jack gnawed his lip and waited.

The plane swooped close to the water, wetting her floats and sending up a great arc of spray, but the attempt was ill timed and a huge wave rose up and threatened to engulf her. She lifted her nose just in time and rose up away from the sea, leaving behind a thick trail of black smoke. The plane climbed, dipped a wing to change direction, then chased a wave. When the wave broke and lost its power, the pilot gently brought the plane down on to the water.

"Let's get over there and pick him out!" shouted Quixote. "We'll have ourselves another hand on deck."

"He's probably even worse luck than this boy here," whined Thomas Fell, pinching Jack's shoulder.

Jack pulled away and, leaning over the rail, stared down at the plane. It was a Berger 17 just like Gadfly's, and there was something else familiar about it, but he couldn't say what it was. As he watched the pilot climb out of the cockpit and douse the engine fire with seawater, the strange feeling grew. He was sure he had seen that plane before.

Thomas Fell threw down a rope. The pilot fixed it to the plane, then nimbly climbed up to the ship's rail where Thomas and Horatio helped him onto the deck.

Once on board, the pilot pulled off his goggles and helmet and let loose a mop of curly red hair. Jack's mouth fell open, his throat dried up, and his palms grew sticky with sweat. It wasn't a man, it was Beryl Faversham, the wonderful aviatrix, the darling of the skies!

"Hello," she said, flashing a bright smile at the twins. "Thanks for fishing me out." Both Thomas and Horatio blushed a good strong raspberry red and studied their shoes.

Jack stared at Beryl. He had never dreamed he'd meet her like this. At home he'd often imagined what he'd say, how he'd act, how he'd impress her with his knowledge of planes, and now here she was in front of him and he couldn't do or say anything clever. And Jack wasn't the only one who was speechless. The entire crew stood with their mouths agape like codfish. Even Quixote was at a loss for words.

Beryl raised an eyebrow. "Does anyone speak English?" she asked.

They all nodded slowly.

"Well, are you ever going to say anything?"

Everybody nodded again.

Beryl was lovely. Her face shone with life and her smile was quick and charming. Jack's insides seemed to melt when she looked at him. And she was looking at him now.

"Hey, I know you, don't I?" she said. Everyone turned and stared at Jack.

He froze like a rabbit in the road.

"Don't know," he mumbled, immediately cursing himself. Why couldn't he have said something clever? Gadfly would have said something clever.

"No, wait, you're Henry Black's son, aren't you? Didn't I read . . . weren't you on the airship with him?" She frowned and hurriedly pulled a folded sheet of newspaper out of her pocket.

"It *is* you," she gasped in amazement. "How on earth did you get here?"

Jack took the paper and stared at the photograph. It was the one of him with his father and Gadfly a week before the launch. The stern look on his father's face reminded Jack of everything that he'd done wrong, of all the promises he'd ever broken, and most of all, of the way he'd disobeyed his father by climbing up the air shaft. He gazed at his excited face in the picture and wondered how he could ever have been so happy.

Jack quickly told Beryl how he'd fallen from the airship and how, by some miracle, he'd survived.

"Did anything happen to the *Belle*?" he asked, hoping

against hope that the voices he'd heard in the air shaft had just been figments of his imagination and nothing more. But Beryl's face grew grave as she unfolded the top part of the newspaper.

GIANT AIRSHIP LOST OVER ARCTIC. FEARS GROW FOR SAFETY OF CREW.

Jack felt as though someone had kicked him in the stomach. He closed his eyes and heard again the strange distorted voices in the air shaft.

"... *the tail fin* ..."

"... *sixteen hundred hours* ..."

Beryl touched him gently on the arm. "We picked up their distress signal four days ago," she said. "We've been searching for them ever since, but they have no means of telling us where they are. They must have lost their navigational instruments in the crash. There's a whole rescue team scouring the area where they ought to have come down, but there's no sign of them there. They must have been blown a long way off course."

Jack heard the voices again.

"*Did you fix the rudder like I told you?*"

"... *it's as tight as a cork in a bottle.*"

The image of Gadfly's anguished face disappearing over the hull of the airship leaped into Jack's mind.

"Gadfly," he cried. "What happened to Gadfly?" He

scanned the newspaper, searching for news of his friend.

He soon found out: it appeared that Gadfly had been testing the *Viper* when the airship had crashed, and no more had been heard of him since. Gadfly was feared lost.

"No!" Jack shook his head. "Gadfly isn't lost. He can't be!" But Jack's heart sank as he spoke.

"Who's in charge here, Jack?" asked Beryl. Jack pointed to Quixote.

Beryl held her hand out to the captain. "Beryl Faversham," she said. "Pleased to meet you."

Quixote didn't exactly blush, but his cheeks looked a little flushed as he took off his cap and shook Beryl's hand.

"Captain Emanuel Quixote at your service," he mumbled with a little bow.

"Is it possible to lift my plane onto your ship?" Beryl asked. "I need to repair the engine and be on my way."

"Yes, of course. Not a problem," he said.

Quixote turned to the engineer and began discussing the best way to lift Beryl's plane out of the water.

Suddenly Jack had an idea. "Look," he said, holding up the sheet of newspaper. "See? I didn't make it up. There *are* such things as airships, and my father and his crew *are* stranded on the polar ice."

Quixote took the newspaper from Jack's hand and stared at the photograph. A muscle twitched in his jaw. Jack pointed at the picture.

"That's my father, there. Now you've got to take me back to the Polar Sea and help me find him. You've got to. We've no time to lose."

"No!" replied Quixote, his eyes glittering. Jack flinched, and the crew fell silent. They didn't look at Jack. They kept their eyes on the deck.

Beryl took a step toward Jack. Quixote glanced up and the angry light in his eyes faded. He cleared his throat and bowed slightly to her.

"We will, of course, assist you in any way we can," he said to Beryl, "so that your . . . er . . . airplane will be . . . er . . . airworthy as soon as possible. But I'm afraid we won't be able to assist in any rescue."

Jack didn't understand. "But your ship is their best chance," he said. "You must go back."

"No," answered Quixote, struggling to keep his voice light. "I can't help your father. I can't afford to risk my ship or my crew by returning to those treacherous waters. Besides, the Polar Sea is a vast area. Perhaps if you knew exactly where your father's airship had landed, we could—"

"But I do!" cried Jack. "I took a reading before I fell. I have it."

Quixote's jaw twitched. "Will this reading tell us exactly where to find your father?"

Jack's eyes shone. "Yes, of course! With an almanac, your navigator can work out the coordinates and—"

"This ship has neither an almanac nor a navigator," Quixote said, handing the newspaper back to Jack. He turned and stared at the horizon. "Therefore, we will not be returning to the Polar Sea. Now don't ask me again."

Jack glared at Quixote. He knew that if his father was in Quixote's position he would do everything in his power to help, almanac or no almanac. And so would Gadfly. Jack had no doubt of that.

Quixote turned to Beryl. "I see you have enough room for two in your machine," he said. "Perhaps, when your airplane is repaired, you will be able to take this boy to find his father."

The crew mumbled in surprise. A look from Quixote silenced them.

Beryl set her hands on Jack's shoulders. "Of course I'll take him," she said. "I only hope I can repair the engine in time for it to be of any use."

Quixote nodded gravely and bowed again. "Our engineer will see that you have everything you need," he said. He turned on his heel, crossed the deck, and disappeared inside his cabin.

Chapter 14

Monster Ahoy!

The engineer rolled up his sleeves, clapped his hands, and began shouting directions at the crew. In no time at all, they had rigged up a series of ropes and pulleys, and Beryl's plane, the *Betsy II*, was hoisted on board and secured to the deck. Beryl immediately set to work dismantling the engine.

Jack watched as Beryl pulled the charred guts of the engine to pieces. It was a real mess. He was about to ask how long she thought repairs might take when Quixote walked up to them.

Jack stared at him in amazement—the captain had brushed his coat and combed his hair. Quixote carefully pushed the propeller a quarter turn so he could get a better look at the engine.

"How long will it take, do you think?" he asked.

Beryl pulled her head out of the housing, tossed the remains of a piston on the deck, and shrugged.

"Can't say yet," she replied, wiping her hands on a rag. "I'm hoping the fire didn't penetrate too far. If we're lucky, it looks worse than it is. If we're unlucky . . ."

Quixote nodded. "I hope you're lucky," he said. "I know you need to be on your way. I've instructed my men to give you all the assistance they can."

"Thank you," replied Beryl. The color rose in Quixote's cheeks, and he bowed again, then returned to his cabin. Jack stared after him and shook his head.

"If he really cared, he'd take us back," he said to Beryl.

"I think he believes it would be putting his own ship and his crew in too much danger," said Beryl gently. "Don't worry, as soon as I get this fixed we can be on our way."

Jack shook his head. "It might be too late by then."

Beryl looked at him. "We'll do our best," she said.

The hiss of white noise suddenly crackled in the air. *Waa-ooii-ee. Waa-ooi-eee,* it wailed.

"Quick!" Beryl said. "It's the radio!" She reached into the cockpit to tune it in. "They broadcast every hour."

Jack jumped up on the step so that he could see into the cockpit.

"It'll come through in a minute," said Beryl as she twisted the dial and turned up the volume. The hissing crackle broke into words.

Waaa Weeee aaaa Waaaa . . . "day Mayday . . . This is Captain Black of the Bellerophon . . . Mayday . . . Mayday . . ."

Jack suddenly felt ice cold all over. He knew that the desperate crackling voice on the radio was his father's, but he could hardly believe it. He sounded so old and tired, so very nearly beaten. Jack felt numb and his head began to ache. He closed his eyes and listened carefully to his father's words.

". . . the crew remain in good spirits, though our supplies are running out. We have been told that the coordinates I have been relaying are incorrect and that searches in those areas have been fruitless. I cannot give our position because we have lost our navigational instruments and . . . "

Jack's eyes snapped open. "How could I have been so stupid?" he cried. "The radio!" His eyes shone as he tried to make Beryl understand. "We can use your radio and give my father the last reading I took. He can work out where they are from that and tell the rescue parties where to find them!"

But Beryl shook her head. "We can't," she said, reaching into the cockpit and lifting the radio's handset from its hook. It had been completely destroyed by the fire.

Jack slid off the side of the plane. "If only Gadfly wasn't lost," he said. "Maybe then there'd be some hope."

"Humph!" muttered Beryl, turning back to the ruined

engine and yanking out a fistful of wires. "Lost? I bet he's lost."

"What do you mean?" Jack asked.

"Oh, nothing," she answered.

Jack was about to ask her again when suddenly Quixote cried, "Monster off the port bow!"

Jack stared openmouthed as the crew darted across the deck to grab hold of lifelines and tie themselves to the rail. A few hundred yards to port the sea bubbled in a circle of white foam as big as a field.

"What's happening?" cried Beryl.

"Grab on to something quick!" yelled Thomas, hurrying past them.

"Tie yourselves to the mast!" cried Simon. Jack and Beryl ran to the mainmast and tied themselves to the fife rail.

Only Quixote remained unbound.

Suddenly the air rang with strange howls. *Aawoooooo! Aawoooooo!*

The captain braced himself against the rail. "Come on, my beauty, show yourself," he muttered. Then he cried, "Here she comes!"

A mountainous wave rose as high as the yardarm, and then fell away to reveal the monster.

It was nothing like Jack had expected. He thought all sea monsters had spiny tentacles and bloodred eyes. But this monster looked more like a giant manatee. Her bright friendly eyes twinkled from beneath folds of sleek, wet fur. She was nearly as long as the *Hyperion*, and as she dived beneath the ship, she flipped up her tail in a salute.

Quixote ran across the deck and reached the far rail just as the monster lifted herself out of the water. She waggled her head from side to side, then disappeared again. This time she came up at the stern.

"Hold on!" yelled Quixote. Everyone tightened their grip on the ropes as the monster slapped both her flippers down on the water. A huge wave lifted the ship and carried it across the ocean. Jack was glad he was tied to the rail or he would have been thrown overboard. Beryl winced as the *Betsy II* strained against her ropes.

The crew laughed like hyenas as the ship scudded across the water. When the ship slowed they had only enough time to catch their breath before the captain yelled, "Hang on! Here she comes again!"

This time the monster lifted her tail out of the water and brought it crashing down with a tremendous slap. The wave it made was five times as big as the other. It lifted the ship and carried it for miles. The *Hyperion* surfed down the wall of water until the wave broke and the ship was drenched in foam. And still the crew laughed.

The monster caught up with them and, laying a flipper across the bowsprit, began to gnaw on the prow.

Quixote grabbed an oar from the skiff.

"Go on, get out of it!" he warned, brandishing the oar.

The monster stopped chewing and stared at him, then ever so slowly inched her muzzle back toward the prow.

"Ah ah ah . . . ," warned Quixote, shaking the oar.

The monster pulled away. But the minute the captain took his eyes off her, she opened her jaws just the tiniest bit and gingerly began to nibble. The captain brought the oar down smartly on her nose.

"No!" he said. He struck only once, but that was enough. The monster whimpered and backed away.

"Come on, I hardly touched you," the captain said. "And you were told not to do that anyway."

With a snuffle the monster rolled over like a puppy that wants its belly to be scratched. Quixote shook his head and laughed and reached out with the oar, but suddenly the ship lurched to one side.

Quixote clung to the rail.

"Oh, no," he cried. "Look at the damage you've done this time. Go on, off with you, you damn puppy, sharpening your teeth on my ship!"

The monster whimpered and sank into the deep blue water. The rest of the crew quickly untied themselves and joined Quixote at the rail. The monster's gnawing had cracked the hull. The ship was taking on water by the second and listing badly.

"Thomas and Sky, man the pumps," ordered the captain. "The rest of you, set sail. It's too big a hole to fix at sea. We'll have to take her in. "

At these words Jack's hope rose again. Despite what he'd said, Quixote was taking the ship into port! Wherever they landed, however remote they were, he'd find a way to get in touch with the rescue parties.

Quixote stared at the empty horizon and held his forefinger up to the wind. "It's fortunate," he said, "that we're less than a day from Welkin Isle."

"Fortunate indeed," whispered Mr. Treacle in Jack's ear. "There's no other place he'd put into, not even if our lives depended on it."

Jack's hope crumpled. Welkin Isle! That wasn't a port. It wasn't even land. It was no more than a legend, a ship's graveyard shrouded in mystery. It was an isolated rock in the middle of the ocean, famous only for the ships that had come to grief on its shores.

Chapter 15

The Way to Welkin Isle

All hands on board the *Hyperion* worked through the night. They set the sails and took turns pumping out the water that seeped in through the hole in the prow. They were some fifty miles from Welkin Isle when they first felt the winds pulling them toward that mysterious island. It was as if an invisible thread had wound itself around the ship and was drawing it steadily across the water.

At dawn the island was in sight. It was a terrible, inhospitable place, rising from the sea like a vast, jagged monument. Sheer, impenetrable cliffs, thousands of feet high, leaned like warnings over the swirling waters. There were no beaches, or sandy coves, or inlets that would serve as a harbor. In the shadows of the great cliffs, broken rocks formed a treacherous reef that spiraled out and encircled the island three times. All three rings of the reef were strewn with the rotting hulls of wrecked ships—the legends of Welkin Isle as a ship's graveyard were true. Jack shuddered. He would rather fall from ten more airships than sail into those waters.

As the *Hyperion* sailed toward the island, the wind picked up and caught her firmly in its grip; the ship scudded across the water leaving a great white wake. As she pitched and rolled, water poured in through the hole in her prow. The men at the pump pumped furiously.

"All hands take in the sails!" commanded Quixote. He pointed at Jack. "You! Take over at the pump." Jack ran to the pump at the head of the foredeck. Beryl joined him, and together they relieved Horatio and Eric. The crew hurried up the masts and set to bringing in the sails, but when they'd finished and all the canvas was furled, it seemed to make no difference to the speed of the ship. Sail or no sail, the winds of Welkin Isle still drew the *Hyperion* on.

Quixote kept his eyes on the treacherous reef. Occasionally he gave out gruff instructions to Eric Lamb at the wheel, but for the most part he kept quiet and waited as the ship plowed on. In his hand, he clutched the small brown map that Jack had seen rolled inside the little glass bottle in the captain's cabin.

They were almost at the reef when the wind grew

even stronger. The ship surged forward, cutting through the water like a racing yacht.

"Engines now!" bellowed Quixote as he took over the wheel. "Half steam astern, Mr. Lamb. Let's see if we can get her to slow a little." Quixote steered perilously close to the outer edge of the reef.

Some of the crew held long oars over the side of the ship, ready to push her off if she came too close. Thomas Fell leaned over the front rail and stared into the foaming waters. He held one hand high above his head.

"Steady, steady," he said. "Come now, Tom. You can't be nervous, you've done this many times before. Come on steady—steady—steady . . ." Then suddenly he shouted, "There it is! Now, Captain, now!" and dropped his hand. The captain swung the wheel, and the ship turned straight into the reef.

Jack closed his eyes and waited for the sickening crunch as the *Hyperion* rode onto the reef, but it didn't come. He opened his eyes and saw that they were sailing steadily along a narrow channel of calm blue water. On either side of them, the white waters raged over the reef.

The channel did not lead directly to the island; instead, it ran around the vast cliffs, spiraling along the reef and circling in to meet the island.

"Jack, pump!" cried Beryl. While they'd been watching Thomas, the water had risen almost up to their knees.

The *Hyperion* held a steady course along the narrow channel. Three times they sailed around the island until, at last, they were deep within the shadow of the cliffs.

Now they sailed between the great rocks that had broken off the mountains. Strewn amongst these monoliths lay the last remains of several ships. It was a lonely, gruesome sight.

Quixote stood like a statue at the helm. His eyes shone black. "How goes it, Thomas?" he called to his signalman.

"Steady—as you have her," Thomas replied as he raised his hand once more.

"The *Spanish Lady*, there's the first," Thomas said as they passed a moldering galleon. Her rotting timbers, white with salt, looked like a monstrous, decayed rib cage.

"There's the whaler," he said as they passed a rusted whaling ship with its harpoon bent and useless.

"Here it comes now. Come on, you beauty, there you are," Thomas said, and as they pulled past a jagged tangle of broken bows and masts, he dropped his hand. "Now, Captain, over hard, now!" he cried.

Quixote spun the wheel furiously and slowly the ship turned toward the rock face. The rock was dark and solid and impenetrable. But as the ship turned back on itself in a sharp bobbing circle, Jack saw a narrow corridor open up behind an overlap of rock. It couldn't have been seen from any other angle. The men drew in their poles as the ship slipped inside.

It was as dark as a tomb. The only sounds were the squeak of the pump and the low drone of the ship's engines, cut now to quarter speed. The slow rhythmic pulse beat out the moments as the ship inched forward.

Thomas lit a candle. The flame burned steadily in the darkness like a tiny yellow star. Thomas crawled out along the bowsprit and held the light high.

Suddenly a quick wind blew out the candle. The engines roared as the captain swung the wheel hard to starboard. Jack breathed a sigh of relief. Now, far ahead of them, he saw an end to the darkness—a tiny arch filled with bright golden light.

It wasn't long before the *Hyperion* emerged into a startlingly beautiful lagoon. A white sandy beach encircled turquoise water, coconut palms swayed in the soft breeze, and lush forests smothered the hills. High cliffs towered above the jungle, their ancient faces covered in green vines, and a waterfall cascaded in a fine spray to a stream below, throwing rainbows over the jungle.

On top of the cliff was a wide plateau, and beyond this, rocky, boulder-strewn hills stood guard around the base of the magnificent, steep-sided mountain. The mountain was a deep ancient gray in color, and its peak was cloaked in shifting wraiths of cloud. Jack gazed about him in wonder. It was a glorious place.

"Pump!" cried Beryl, waking Jack from his daze. "Pump!"

Jack looked down and saw that the water was quickly pooling around his legs. He grasped the handle and began to pump for all he was worth.

Chapter 16

Dorothy

When all the water that could be pumped out of the bow had been pumped out, and the *Hyperion* lay quietly at anchor in the calm waters of the lagoon, Jack climbed down from the ship and half swam, half waded to shore. The water of the lagoon was so clear he could see pale white crabs and tiny silver fishes skittering away from his feet.

Jack yawned and with his shoes slung around his neck made his way across the soft, warm sand toward the deep shade of the coconut palm trees. He was exhausted from the hard work and intended to take a nap. Several of the crew were already asleep and snoring on the sand. The Fell twins were singing softly together in their sleep. Jack wandered away from them. He wanted to be alone; he wanted to think. But the moment he lay down in the cool shade of a coconut palm, he fell fast asleep. He was too tired even to dream.

A loud thud close to his head woke him with a start. Jack turned and saw a large green coconut beside him on the sand. He realized if it had landed any closer, it might have killed him! He sat up like a shot and stared into the tall trees. Hundreds of coconuts were clustered in the middle of the dark leaves just waiting to fall. Jack jumped up and ran out onto the unshaded, yet safer, part of the beach.

"I should have warned you not to sleep under those trees," said Beryl as she walked up the beach toward him. She went into the shade and picked up the coconut, then sat down next to Jack. "I need a break— and some breakfast!" she said.

Jack sat down in the sand and stared across the sparkling water at the *Hyperion*.

"Is the *Betsy II* nearly fixed?" he asked.

Beryl shook her head. Taking out her knife, she jabbed two small holes in the top of the coconut.

"I'm sorry, Jack. The damage is worse than I thought. The good news is that the engineer can make replacements for the parts I need; the bad news is that it'll be at least two more days before we're done."

Jack groaned in frustration. Two more days! It didn't sound like very long, but for his father and the crew of the *Belle,* two days could mean the difference between life and death.

"Here, try some of this," said Beryl as she rested the coconut beside him in the sand. But Jack didn't hear her. On the *Hyperion*, Eric Lamb and Sky were dangling over the side of the ship on boatswain's chairs, repairing the hole in the prow, while Quixote sat in the skiff below and pointed out any bits they'd missed. It looked as though the repairs were almost complete.

The *Hyperion* was a fast ship. If Beryl's plane wasn't going to be ready for two days or more, then the *Hyperion* was still the airship crew's best hope. If only he had an almanac and knew how to work out the coordinates! Then he'd know exactly where to find the airship, and Quixote would have to help.

"Come on, Jack," said Beryl, breaking into Jack's thoughts. "You've got to keep your strength up, you know." Jack looked at her blankly. She pointed to the coconut. "There's milk inside."

Jack hadn't realized how thirsty he was until he drank a little of the coconut milk. It was sweet and refreshing, and he liked it so much that he tipped his head back and guzzled it down in one go.

When the milk was gone, Beryl sliced open the coconut and scooped out the flesh. They ate it with their fingers, and the juice ran down their arms.

When they'd finished, Beryl jumped up and shook the sand off her clothes.

"I'd better get back to work," she said. "Try not to

worry, Jack. We'll find your father in time. Really. I'm sure we will."

Jack nodded. Beryl smiled and then turned and hurried across the sand. Jack watched her go. How could Gadfly have thought her anything but lovely? he wondered.

He watched as Quixote waved at Beryl. The captain said something to the men above him, grabbed the oars, and began to row toward the shore. Jack stood and turned away, heading up the beach toward the waterfall.

Farther along the beach Horatio Fell was walking slowly, hunched over as though searching for something in the sand. Every so often he stooped to pick something up. Jack noticed Thomas doing the same thing at the other end of the beach.

Jack bent down and picked up a stone so large it almost covered his palm. He held it to the sun and the light shone through it with a deep ruddy brown glow.

It could be a ruby, he thought, remembering the rough stones the men had used on the ship. He put it in his pocket and continued up the beach. By the time he reached the waterfall, three large rubies clanked together in his pocket.

Jack knelt at the foot of the waterfall and plunged his head into the icy stream. The water was so cold it made his skin tingle. He gasped as he pulled his head out and shook the water from his hair. He wiped his face with his hands, then lay on his back and gazed up through the spray.

Something sparkled at the top of the waterfall. Jack lifted himself onto his elbows. If he didn't know better, he'd swear it was the sun reflecting off a lens. . . . But how could that be, on this deserted island?

Suddenly Jack felt something smack him on the chest. He glanced down and saw a small gray pebble lying there. While he was staring at it, another one pinged against the side of his head.

"Hey!" Jack spun around. Behind him was a wall of dense green jungle. As he watched, another pebble flew out and caught him right on the nose. "Ow!" Jack cried.

A small red-faced monkey was grinning at him through the leaves of a tree. In his little hand he held his ammunition, a whole cache of pebbles. Jack noticed that the monkey had only one eye, the other closed in a permanent mocking wink.

"Why, you little . . . ," cried Jack, jumping up. He picked up his shoes, and, holding them by the laces, swung them at the monkey. It screamed, threw the whole handful of stones at once, then turned tail and scampered into the trees.

Jack chased after it through the forest. Again and again he almost caught the monkey's tail, but the little beast jumped up into the trees and laughed at him through the leaves. Jack swung his shoes at him again, but the monkey just scurried to the top of the tree. Jack finally gave up. He bent over with his hands on his knees. He was out of breath and disappointed, and worst of all he suddenly realized he was lost.

Remembering something he had once read about tropical millipedes that could kill a man in less than three minutes with just one bite, Jack put on his shoes. He pushed through the undergrowth and eventually came to a small clearing. It wasn't a natural break in the forest; the trees and undergrowth had been cut back. At the other side of the clearing was the beginning of a path, which looked as though it might lead down to the beach. Jack would have hurried over, but in the center of the clearing were three wooden boxes—and they were humming loudly. Jack was stepping toward them when a shriek stopped him in his tracks.

"Kippperwayfromthebeees! Kippperwayfromthebeees!"

Racing toward him was a creature unlike anything he had ever seen. It was swaddled from head to foot in rough cloth; it had no face, just a blank wall of sacking with two slits for eyeholes; and in one hand it held a bunch of smoldering sticks that trailed thick smoke behind it.

"Kippperwayfromthebeees!" it screamed again as it grabbed Jack's arm and dragged him back into the jungle.

"Did you not hear me shouting for you to keep away from the bees?" asked a clear voice from behind the sackcloth. "They're about to swarm! Still, better a quick drag through the forest than an attack from a hundred bad-tempered bees."

The creature pulled off its veil and hat to reveal an old lady with bright white hair tied in a neat bun and a face as brown and wrinkled as an old apple.

"Hello," she said. "I'm Dorothy Dobson, castaway and sole tenant of this glorious place. I see that you've already met my friend Nelson." Dorothy reached out and picked a small pebble from Jack's hair, then she whistled two short notes and a long one. With a gleeful screech the little monkey dropped from the trees, scampered across the clearing, and climbed onto Dorothy's shoulder. He grinned cheekily at Jack, then reached into Dorothy's pocket, pulled out a plum, turned it in his little hands, and bit into it.

"Be nice, Nelly. We have company. No throwing things. Now, where were we? Oh, yes." Dorothy smiled again and held out her hand to Jack. "I'm Dorothy, this is Nelson—or Nelly—and who, may I ask, are you?"

Jack liked this beekeeping castaway instantly. He grasped her outstretched hand.

"My name's Jack Black," he said. "I arrived on that ship down there in the lagoon, but I didn't . . ."

Dorothy gasped, and her face lit up like a candle. "There's only one ship I know of that can find its way to this sweet shore. Quixote's here, Nelly!" Dorothy laughed, and Nelly jabbered and started to pull Dorothy's hair out of the neat bun.

"You know him?" asked Jack.

"I do, indeed. He comes to visit me when the winds blow him this way." Dorothy reached up and tried to catch the monkey's hands. "Nelly! Behave!"

Dorothy gave Jack an exasperated look and went on. "After I was shipwrecked here, I drew a map and put it in a bottle, and the tide carried it out to sea. The map showed how a small boat could get through the reef and into the lagoon without ending up like those wrecks outside. Your friend Quixote found my map. I never expected anyone to make it through in a full-size ship, but that's Quixote for you. Every year or so he brings me supplies and collects gemstones from the beach. Oh, I do so enjoy having visitors!"

Dorothy put her hand to her head and tried to smooth her hair back down, but the monkey had made a proper mess of it. A look of horror swept over her face.

"Great heavens," she cried. "What am I thinking? Visitors, and look at the state I'm in! We'll need firewood, and I must get changed."

"Can I help?" offered Jack.

"Yes, you can!" she said, smiling broadly. "You could fetch the wood. There's a basket and an ax halfway up the hill. At the top you'll find a dead tree. You can't miss it, it's the only dead one. Just chop it up and bring as much wood as you can carry to the beach. Follow this path all the way down, and you'll soon come to my cottage. Keep going and you'll be back at the beach before you know it."

With Nelly still clinging to her hair, Dorothy set off down the path. Jack started up the hill. He hadn't gone more than a few paces when Dorothy came chasing after him.

"Here, you'd better take this," she said, pulling a pistol from her belt and handing it to Jack. "If you see any large snakes, shoot at them and they'll go away. I'll see you at the beach. Oh, and Jack?" she called, trying once more to disentangle Nelly's little hands from her hair. "It's very nice to meet you!"

Nelly jabbered as though in agreement and then clutched at the bright white hair once more as Dorothy set off at a brisk trot down the path.

Chapter 17

Snake in the Grass

Jack found the ax and the basket exactly where Dorothy had said he would and carried them to the top of the hill. There the tall grass rustled in the breeze and butterflies danced in the sun. Somewhere behind the curtain of grass the waterfall thundered.

Jack had no trouble finding the dead tree. Much of it had already been chopped up. He began to pick up the pieces and put them in the basket. It was as he was crouching down that he heard the whistling. Jack picked up Dorothy's gun and listened harder. At first he thought it was just the water cascading down the cliff, but as he listened, he could make out a tune—a very familiar tune.

Yes, we have no bananas, we have no bananas today.

There was only one person Jack knew who whistled like that! But it couldn't be, could it?

It was coming from the waterfall. Jack stole softly toward it. The tall grass stopped twenty yards from the cliff edge; the open ground beyond was hard, uneven clay studded with rocks. Jack peered through the grass and saw something that sent his brain reeling.

Wallace Gadfly lay at the edge of the cliff, peering down at the lagoon through a pair of field glasses.

Gadfly! thought Jack with a rush of happiness. Gadfly wasn't lost. He was here! He was alive! Jack almost cried out for joy, but he restrained himself. It would be more fun to give his friend a real surprise.

He sneaked out of the grass as silently as a snake and crept up behind Gadfly.

"What are you doing there, ya varmint?" he growled, knocking Gadfly's foot with his toe.

The whistling stopped and Gadfly's shoulders shot up to his ears, but he didn't turn around. Jack kicked him a little harder.

"Go on, ya varmint, show yourse—"

Suddenly a fat, sweaty hand clamped over his mouth and a heavy arm encircled his body, pinning his arms to his sides. Gadfly twisted around and in a flash snatched Dorothy's gun away. He pointed it with a cool and steady aim at Jack's head.

Jack squealed. For a moment he wasn't sure that the

person in front of him was Gadfly at all. The hard face with taut bloodless lips and burning eyes didn't look like the face of his friend.

"Come up here to spy on us, did you, you little rat?" Gadfly said.

Jack tipped back his head and saw Blunt's grim features scowling down at him. He bit Blunt's pudgy hand. The mechanic yelped and pulled his hand away.

"Gadfly!" Jack shouted. "Gadfly, it's me, Jack!"

Blunt raised his fist.

"Wait!" Gadfly said, leaning forward and narrowing his eyes. "It can't be," he said under his breath. "I saw Jack fall."

Gadfly dropped the pistol on the ground, grabbed Jack by the shoulders, and pulled him away from Blunt. "It *is* you!" he gasped. His eyes opened wide and his face relaxed into a smile. "I can't believe it! Jack! How?" He let go of Jack and rubbed his forehead. "I must be dreaming. Hallucinating. How did you get here? Are you real?"

"You don't know how glad I am to see you," whispered Jack. "There *was* a bomb on the *Belle*." Jack snatched up the pistol, then spun around and pointed it at Blunt.

"I told you I heard him, I told you!" Jack said. The heavy pistol wobbled in his hands. Blunt narrowed his eyes and spat.

"Jack, no," Gadfly laughed nervously. "Give me the gun. There wasn't any bomb, that was just your imagination."

"But the *Belle* crashed," Jack said. "I know she crashed."

"Yes, she did, Jack," Gadfly said. "But there was no explosion. Believe me, I saw her fall."

Jack lowered the gun. Gently Gadfly took it from him.

"Blunt and I were out testing the *Viper* at the time," Gadfly explained. "I flew off to fetch help, but, as you can see, we had some trouble."

Gadfly pointed back toward the grass, and Jack saw the remains of the *Viper*'s propeller with its yellow and black stripes lying on the ground; it had been snapped in two. Beside it lay a rough attempt at a replica carved from the wood of the dead tree.

"The *Belle*'s crash was an accident, Jack," Gadfly continued. "Accidents were bound to happen under the circumstances."

"What do you mean?" asked Jack.

Gadfly shrugged and turned back toward the lagoon. "What's that plane down there on the ship?" he asked.

"Beryl Faversham's," said Jack. "What did you mean about accidents were bound to happen? What circumstances?"

"Then it *is* a Berger 17. It was hard to tell with all the

damage." Gadfly's eyes glittered. "The propeller looks sound. If we could just get that, we could be on our way. But," he added with a sigh, "Faversham isn't the type to let me have it, even though we could get help to your father faster. She can be very selfish when she chooses. But you could get it for us, couldn't you?"

Jack stared down at Beryl's plane. Parts of the engine were still spread out all over the deck.

"Come on, Jack," urged Gadfly. "Who knows how long it'll be before her plane is able to fly? If you help me, your father'll be home safe before you know it. What do you say?"

Jack frowned. "Tell me what you meant."

"When?"

"Before, when you said that accidents were bound to happen. What did you mean?"

"Oh that," Gadfly said softly. "I didn't want to tell you this, but the reason the *Belle* went down . . . Well, it was because . . ."

"Because what?" asked Jack anxiously.

"Oh, Jack. When your father heard about you falling, he took it pretty hard. He wasn't himself. We tried to persuade him to stay in his cabin. We'd flown into some bad weather, and we didn't think he should be making difficult decisions when he'd had such a shock. But you know your father, Jack. No one can tell him what to do."

Jack frowned. "My father is the best airship captain

in the world," he said. "He's always careful. He wouldn't risk his men. . . ."

"I know, Jack," said Gadfly. "Under normal circumstances he could have flown through those winds as easy as pie. But think about it, Jack. After what had happened . . . After you . . . Well, he wasn't himself."

"You're saying it was my fault . . . ," Jack whispered. "It was my fault that the *Belle* went down."

"Jack, it was nobody's fault," Gadfly said. "And even if it was, the important thing now is finding a way to help those poor men. If you get me that propeller, I promise you, I swear on my honor, we'll get help to your father."

Jack looked into Gadfly's shining face.

"What about the radio in the *Viper?*" Jack asked. "I have the last reading taken from the *Belle*. We could radio it to the rescue parties. We could . . ."

Gadfly shook his head.

"It's no use, Jack. I took the radio out so that the *Viper* would be lighter for testing the trapeze. No, the only hope for your father now is if you get me that propeller."

Gadfly held out the pistol. Jack took it and stuck it in his belt.

"Meet me halfway up the path at first light," Jack said. "I'll have the propeller for you." He paused and took a deep breath. "You'll take me with you, won't you?"

Gadfly smiled. "Of course, I will. I promise.

Everything will be all right now, Jack. Everything will be fine."

Jack nodded. "I'd best be getting back," he said, "or they'll wonder what's happened to me."

But as he turned away, a strange, low rumbling began that quickly grew louder. The earth began to tremble, and the mountain itself seemed to shake! Gadfly's binoculars bounced along the ground and flew over the edge of the cliff. Jack lost his footing and stumbled, falling facedown on the ground.

Then, as suddenly as it had begun, the shaking stopped. Jack raised his head. A whisper of dark smoke coiled from the top of the mountain and drew an ominous line across the setting sun.

"You'd better hurry," said Gadfly as he helped Jack pick up the firewood. "It's getting late. The sooner you get the propeller, the sooner we can get help to your father." Jack nodded and, carrying the basket, hurried down the trail.

The basket of wood was heavy, and by the time he reached the clearing with the beehives Jack's arms needed a rest. He put the basket on the ground for a moment and stared at the gloomy forest.

He didn't want to steal Beryl's propeller, but Gadfly was right—it was the fastest way to get help to his father. But if he stole it, was he condemning Beryl to a life on board the *Hyperion?* If he didn't, was he condemning his father to death?

Jack heard Gadfly's words. *Every man must make his own way in the world.* They were wise words, but for the first time they didn't help him. What was he going to do?

As he stood there wrestling with the problem, he realized that somewhere nearby, someone was crying. Jack peered through the trees. In the gathering gloom, he could just make out Dorothy standing beside the remains of a small log cabin. One wall was still standing, but the rest was a jumble of tree trunks pointing in all directions like spilled matches. Dorothy stared forlornly at the mess while Nelson scampered back and forth across the rubble.

Chapter 18

By the Fire

Nelson pulled a book from the rubble and carried it to Dorothy. She took it and hugged it to her chest.

Jack picked up the basket of wood and walked past the beehives to join her beside the ruins. "Was this your house?" he asked.

Dorothy blinked at him. "It was my home," she said. "I built it seventeen years ago."

Dorothy smoothed the tears off her face with her fingers and then gently set a bamboo stool the right way up and sat down.

"I shouldn't be so sentimental," she said. "I can always build another house." Then she saw the basket full of wood Jack had brought, and she smiled. "Oh, well done!" she said.

"You should have your gun back, too," Jack said as he

reached for the pistol at his belt. It wasn't there. "That's strange, it must have fallen out during the earthquake. I'd better go back and . . ."

"Oh, don't worry about that now," Dorothy said. "Go and get it in the morning. It'll be easier to find in the daylight."

Jack stared up the dark path. No matter what Gadfly said, he still didn't trust Blunt, and he didn't want to think about what might happen if Blunt found Dorothy's gun.

The yellow light of a lantern came through the trees toward them, and presently Quixote appeared on the far side of the tumbled-down house. Nelly screeched and scampered onto Dorothy's shoulder.

"Gregor Ladislav Lavinovich, what a mess!" said Quixote. He hurried over to Dorothy. "Are you all right?" he asked.

"Oh, Emanuel! I'm fine," she said, disentangling Nelly's hands from her hair. "Don't fuss."

"How long has this been going on?" asked Quixote. "These tremors, and the mountain smoking like that. You know what's coming, don't you?"

"Oh, you worry too much," Dorothy said, getting to her feet. "This island's like me, good for a few more years. I was just coming to join you on the beach."

"I thought you might want to dress for dinner, seeing as you have company," Quixote said. He smiled and held out a crumpled ball of blue cloth. Dorothy gasped as the ball unraveled to reveal the beautiful silk dress.

"I hope you paid for this," she said, obviously pleased.

"I gave the captain two big sapphires in exchange. I have some books for you, too, but there doesn't seem to be any point bringing them up here, seeing as you'll be sailing with us in the morning now that the *Hyperion* is repaired."

Dorothy gave him a long look and then smiled. "I'm much too happy to see you to argue about this tonight. We'll talk about it tomorrow. You and Jack go on ahead and get the fire started. I want to get changed."

By the time Dorothy joined them on the beach the fire was burning nicely and supper was almost ready. Sky had wrapped fish in palm-tree leaves and stuck them deep into the fire. They took only a few minutes to cook.

Dorothy looked beautiful in the blue dress. The crew fussed over her, and Jack could tell she was terribly fond of all of them. Simon spread his coat for her to sit on, and Thomas Fell brought her fish to eat. Dorothy smiled and handed tidbits to Nelson, who sat by her side.

Beryl sat down next to Jack and handed him some fish. Jack couldn't look at her. He felt terribly guilty about what he was planning to do. But if he took the propeller to Gadfly the rescue parties could be with his father before Beryl's plane was even ready to fly. *If only I could tell Beryl about it,* Jack thought.

He glanced at her out of the corner of his eye. "I wish Gadfly was here," he said, trying to sound casual. "He'd be able to help."

Beryl said nothing. The firelight flickered over her face.

"You don't like him, do you?" Jack said.

Beryl shrugged and stared across the water. "I don't trust him. There was some awkwardness a year or so back. I was competing against him in a race, and I won fair and square. The problem was he didn't agree with the judges' decision. He tried to say I'd cheated. It made for a lot of bad feeling."

Jack threw his fish bones onto the fire and watched the sparks rise into the sky. "Gadfly must have had a good reason to think that way," he said.

"Must he?" replied Beryl. She looked as though she was about to say more, but she stopped herself and smiled at Jack. "Oh, don't mind me. I was just annoyed at the time. It put a damper on the whole joy of winning my first race. Look, he's your friend and you know him better than I do. I have to get back to the *Betsy II*. I wish there was a way to get it fixed faster, but if there is, I don't know it." She stuffed a last piece of fish in her mouth and jumped up.

"Beryl . . . I . . . er . . . ," Jack began.

Beryl looked at him expectantly. Jack desperately wanted to tell her that Gadfly was alive and on the island,

and that he was his father's best hope. But he couldn't find the words. He knew now what Beryl thought of Gadfly. She'd never let him have the *Betsy II*'s propeller. Jack's heart fell. He would have to steal it after all.

"What is it, Jack?" she asked.

"Nothing," he said. "Nothing at all."

The crew of the *Hyperion* had finished their meal and were lounging around the fire.

"Well?" asked Dorothy, smiling at them. "What fine adventures have you been on since last you were here? I see you've got a new shipmate. Come on, I want to hear your stories."

And then the storytelling began. Sky told a long and complicated tale about a pirate ship they'd fought in the southern seas. Then Eric Lamb recounted the time they'd been caught in a storm where the waves had been as big as mountains and they'd been lifted so high they thought they'd be crushed against the clouds.

All the crew were excellent storytellers, and they were enjoying themselves immensely. Their stories grew longer and more preposterous as the night wore on and were full of sea monsters and witches and mermaids. Dorothy oohed and aahed and laughed in all the right places, and clapped her hands when they'd finished a tale, but Jack didn't enjoy them at all. He sat on the edge of the circle only half listening. He was busy with his thoughts of what he had promised to do.

But his ears pricked up when he heard his name. Mr. Treacle was telling the story of the fish boy again.

"Jack, here," he said with a hiccup, "is really a fish boy. He was thrown out of the sea by a vengeful father and made to live—"

"That is such rubbish!" Jack burst out. "Why won't any of you tell the truth? All of you know I fell from an airship and landed on the *Hyperion,* and all of you know it happened while you were being chased by that warship . . . by the . . . the . . ." In his mind's eye, he saw again the seven funnels, each bearing a letter of the name. The men around the fire held their breath. Eric Lamb shook his head, warning Jack to keep quiet. But suddenly Jack had it.

". . . the *Nemesis,*" he said, and the sound of that name rang in the air like a death knell.

A cloud passed over the moon, and every creature in the jungle fell silent. The crew slipped away from the fire. Only Quixote, sitting in the shadows, and Dorothy beside him, did not move. Dorothy reached out and touched the captain's arm.

"He's only a boy," she said gently. "He doesn't know any better."

But Quixote stood up and walked through the fire toward Jack, not even noticing when the hot embers scorched the leather of his boots and filled the air with the acrid smell of burning polish.

Jack stood up to face him. The captain reached down and took hold of Jack's collar, then lifted him up till their eyes were on the same level.

"If you ever mention that name again," said Quixote, "it will be the last sound you ever make. Do you understand?"

Quixote's eyes burned with a fierce, terrifying light.

"Yes," stammered Jack in a strangled whisper. He had no doubt that Quixote would do as he said. But as he stared into the captain's eyes, he saw a flicker of something else, something buried deep beneath the anger and the hate. Jack couldn't say what it was, but for a fleeting moment it was there, and it was as raw and as awful as death.

Quixote dropped Jack on the sand and then disappeared into the shadows.

Dorothy remained by the fire staring at the crackling flames. She sat as still and as calm as a rock. Jack was still, too, but he was far from calm. He felt very hot inside, and his hatred for Quixote was matched only by his fear. His one consolation was knowing that soon he would be away from him, from the *Hyperion*, from this island, and—he hung his head—far, far away from Beryl. But he promised himself that one day he would hunt down the *Hyperion* and rescue her. Jack kicked a log back into the fire, and a shower of sparks shot up into the air.

"He's not a cruel man at heart," Dorothy said softly.

"But his ghosts pursue him wherever he goes."

Jack didn't understand what she meant. He rubbed his neck where his collar had chafed it raw.

"Will you walk me home, Jack?" asked Dorothy. She cradled Nelson in the crook of her arm like a baby and held her free hand toward Jack. "Lend me your shoulder to lean on. I've grown stiff from sitting still so long."

Jack helped her to her feet and together they made their way up the beach.

"There are many mysteries on that ship," said Dorothy, nodding at the *Hyperion* as they walked. "Eric, Sky, even Treacle all have their secrets locked in their hearts. The Fell brothers, too. Long ago they fought over a girl. Now they each pretend the other doesn't exist. I think they want to be brothers again, but each is too proud to be the first to break the silence." Dorothy shook her head. "It's a terrible shame. They've voices like angels, but they only ever sing in their sleep."

"Where will you sleep?" asked Jack when they reached the ruined hut.

"Under the stars," replied Dorothy. "Good night, Jack. Keep out of Quixote's way for a while."

Chapter 19

Dawn Flight

It was still dark when Jack unwound himself from his sand-speckled blanket. He hadn't really slept. His mind was too full. He sat up and looked around. Behind him the mountain peak glowed with a strange orange light. Across the water, he could just make out the silhouette of the *Hyperion*. It was quiet and dark. He looked down the beach and saw Beryl asleep on the far side of the fire, her bright hair sticking out over the top of her blanket.

Jack crept down to the water's edge and slipped silently into the lagoon. The water was strangely warm, so warm that it almost made him gasp. It was like swimming in soup. When he reached the ship, he found the skiff moored to the ladder. He clung there and listened to the water lapping against the side of the ship. If the skiff was here, someone had to be on board the *Hyperion*. Jack hesitated. Who could it be? The sky was growing pale, and Gadfly would be waiting for him. Jack had to get that propeller. Quietly he started up the ladder.

As he climbed over the rail, a great snore erupted in the silence. Jack froze. It was coming from the *Betsy II*. Jack tiptoed to the cockpit and peered over the rim. Mr. Treacle was fast asleep in the passenger seat.

Jack left the cook to his sugary dreams and silently reached into Beryl's tool bag. He took out a spanner, fit it around one of the eight nuts that held the propeller in place, took a deep breath, and tried to turn it. The nut wouldn't budge. It was screwed down tight. Jack tried again. This time he got a better grip and pushed down firmly on the spanner, but, again, nothing happened. He took another breath, gritted his teeth, and tried again. Still nothing. He was beginning to sweat, and his fingers were aching from the effort. He let go first with one hand and then the other so that he could flex his fingers. He gripped the spanner again and took another deep breath. This time he didn't hold his breath. Instead, he let it out in a long, steady stream. This time, the nut began to turn.

Once he had the knack, he quickly loosened each nut one after the other. Then, laying the spanner on the deck, he spun the nuts off with his fingers, dropping each into his pocket.

Next came the propeller itself. Jack carefully eased it off the plane. It was heavier than he'd imagined, and he staggered under the weight. He leaned it against the rail, tied a rope around it, and lowered it gently over the side into the skiff. Next he fetched the sextant from the forecastle. Then he climbed down into the skiff and pushed off from the side of the ship.

As quietly as possible, Jack fitted the oars in the oarlocks, slipped their blades into the water, and pulled. The little boat slid quietly through the water, but the oarlocks squeaked as they turned. Jack didn't want to risk waking the sleepers on the beach. Carefully he lifted the oars out one at a time and rested them against the gunwales of the skiff. It was more difficult to row that way, but it was much quieter.

Jack rowed toward the stream. There, the roar of the waterfall covered the sound of him dragging the boat onto the beach. When the boat was fast, he hoisted the propeller onto his shoulder and started up the hill. By now the sky was fully light, and Jack found it easy enough to climb up the hill. The propeller soon grew heavy, and the blade dug deep into his shoulder. He was relieved when he saw Gadfly rushing down the hill to meet him.

"Well done, Jack," said Gadfly, taking the propeller and hoisting it onto his own shoulder as if it weighed no more than a matchstick. He ruffled Jack's hair. "Well done! I knew you could do it. We'd better hurry before your shipmates wake and find this missing. Come on."

At the top of the hill Gadfly plowed on into the tall grass.

"How do you like this for a natural runway?" he asked. The plain spread out before them, flat and wide. It was almost a perfect landing strip, but only almost. It looked a little too short for a plane to be able to get up enough speed to take off. Jack knew that if Gadfly had managed to land the *Viper* with a broken propeller on a strip so short, he would certainly be able to take off again, but it wouldn't be easy. Gadfly would have to race toward the waterfall, shoot over the cliff, and hope that he had enough speed to fly. Jack bit his lip. He knew his extra weight wouldn't help.

The *Viper* stood at the far end of the plain, and it cheered Jack's heart to see her.

When they reached her, Gadfly carefully lifted the propeller onto her nose. Jack took the nuts out of his pocket and started to spin them into place. "Four . . . five . . . six . . ."

As Jack spun the last nut into place, Blunt lumbered out of the tall grass and hurried toward the plane.

"They're on to us," he gasped. "They're on their way."

"Jack, my toolbox is under the seat in the front cockpit," Gadfly said. "Fetch me a spanner. Hurry."

As Jack leaned into the cockpit and felt beneath the

seat for the toolbox, he heard a faint hissing sound. He stared at the instrument panel and saw the radio beneath it. There was a radio after all! Jack turned up the volume.

Weeee waaaaa weeeoooooeeeee . . . , it crackled. Then came his father's voice: ". . . sixth day since our first Mayday signal."

There was a pause, an awful, hollow pause. His father sounded so much weaker. "Our supplies are almost finished."

Another pause. Jack swallowed hard and grabbed the handset. "Papa! Papa . . . Can you hear me?"

"This is Captain Black of the *Bellerophon* . . ."

"Papa, it's me! Jack! Can you hear me?"

"Jack? . . . Jack? . . ." His father's voice crackled into silence.

"Papa? We're going to get help. We'll have someone with you soon. Papa, this is the last reading I took from the airship. It's . . ." Jack stood up and scrabbled in the sextant case to get the notebook.

As he turned around, he saw Gadfly hit Blunt on the back of the head with the butt of Dorothy's gun. Blunt groaned and crumpled to the ground. Jack stared at Gadfly in horror.

Gadfly looked up at Jack. "I had to!" he said. "He wasn't willing to be left behind. We can't afford any extra weight when we go over that cliff."

"Jack . . . hello? Jack . . . are you there? Jack?" His

father's voice crackled on the radio. Jack turned back to the notebook in his hand.

"Papa, yes . . . the reading I took, it's . . ."

Gadfly leaped onto the wing, yanked the handset out of Jack's hand, and jumped into the cockpit.

"Why did you stop me?" cried Jack.

"There isn't time," Gadfly said. "Look!"

Two figures were running across the plain. It was Beryl and Quixote.

"Get her started," urged Gadfly. "We'll radio your father as soon as we're airborne. Hurry!"

Jack ran to the front of the plane and grasped the propeller with both hands.

"Jack, don't!" cried Beryl.

"Do it, Jack!" yelled Gadfly. "This is the only way to save your father. Come on!"

Jack looked at his friend. He looked like the same old Gadfly.

Jack swung the propeller down hard. It caught the first time, and the engine roared into life.

"I knew you could do it," cheered Gadfly as he steered the plane around to face the waterfall. Jack dived out of the way and rolled on the grass.

"Wait!" he screamed, scrambling to his feet. But Gadfly revved the engine, and the plane set off across the plateau.

"No!" Jack cried. "You promised to take me with you!"

He ran and hurled himself onto the wing of the plane.

"Get off, Jack!" yelled Gadfly. "She'll never make it with both of us."

The plane was now less than fifty feet from the waterfall and picking up speed. Jack clung to the wing and clawed his way to the cockpit. He snatched at Gadfly's sleeve and clung to it.

"You've got to take me with you!" Jack cried against the gathering wind.

"We'd never make it!" Gadfly shouted. "Now get off, for pity's sake, or neither of us will be in any state to rescue anyone."

Gadfly shoved Jack hard in the chest. Jack lost his hold, fell off the wing, and bounced along the rough ground.

Then the *Viper* disappeared over the edge of the cliff. There was a terrible silence as though the engine had cut out. Jack rolled to the edge and peered down. He watched the yellow plane disappear into the misty spray of the waterfall.

Gadfly wasn't going to make it. He wouldn't be able to pull her up in time. Jack pressed his forehead against the warm, stony ground, waiting for the crash.

But suddenly the engine screamed back to life, and the yellow plane burst out of the spray in a vertical climb, soaring to safety.

Gadfly had been right; he would never have made it

with Jack—or Blunt—on board. But why had Gadfly lied to him about the radio? The radio worked, and Gadfly had said he'd seen where the *Belle* had come down. Why hadn't he informed the rescue parties? Surely he could have done that. Jack shook his head. He didn't understand.

Chapter 20

The End of an Island

Beryl and Quixote ran up to Jack and stood beside him as the *Viper* vanished into the distant clouds. Beryl didn't say anything. There was no need. Jack felt bad enough already.

As he got to his feet, the earth began to shake, and he teetered on the edge of the cliff, his arms flailing. Beryl grabbed him and pulled him back to safety. The shaking stopped.

"I think we'd better get back to the beach," said Quixote, "before . . . oh!"

This time the shaking was more violent. The ground moved like a wave, and the mountain shuddered.

"Look!" cried Jack. "Look!"

The mountain's craggy peak had cracked open, revealing a fiery orange heart. Black smoke poured from the broken crest, turning the sky dark and blotting out the sun. A stream of red-hot lava spilled over the mountaintop and poured down the slope. It looked like the end of the world.

"Let's go!" yelled Beryl.

She hurried across the shaking ground with Jack and Quixote close behind. They staggered down the path toward the beach while the land around them heaved.

Chaos reigned on the beach. The men were scrambling to get everything back to the *Hyperion*—everything, including Dorothy. Quixote, Beryl, and Jack ran down to the skiff, where Dorothy was arguing with Eric Lamb.

"Will you tell him I'm not going?" she said to Quixote. "This is still my island, my home, and you can't make me leave!" Nelson clung to her shoulder and bared his teeth at Eric.

"I'll find you another island," promised Quixote. "You've got to come with us. It's your only chance!"

"No!" said Dorothy. Suddenly there was a thunderous crack as though the whole earth had split wide open. Half the cliff slid into the lagoon. Nelly shrieked and scampered toward the skiff. Dorothy met Quixote's eyes.

"All right," she said, hopping into the boat. Beryl climbed in beside her and reached out for Jack, but he was looking at the *Betsy II*, propellerless on the deck.

"You go on without me!" he said. "I'll be back in a minute!" He started to run back up the beach.

"Jack, where are you going?" Beryl cried after him.

"Come back, Jack!" called Dorothy. "Come back, there isn't time!"

Jack ran toward the waterfall. The smoky air burned the back of his throat as he scrambled up the path. The mountain roared again, and the great crack widened another hundred feet. Fireballs spewed from the heart of the rock and crashed down into the depths of the jungle. Trees and undergrowth burst into flame.

Jack ran on. His only thought was to find the *Viper*'s broken propeller. At the top of the path he saw the yellow-and-black-striped piece of wood lying on the hard clay and snatched it up. But it was only one half. Where was the rest of it? He hunted frantically. There was another terrific rumble from the belly of the mountain. Rocks shot into the air, and the smoky sky grew bright with fireballs. The river of lava had reached the far end of the plateau. There was no time. If the mountain fell, the corridor through the rock would be sealed forever. There would be no way out.

Clasping the broken propeller, Jack hurried to the path.

Suddenly Blunt stumbled out of the tall grass and blocked his way. The mechanic looked dazed. His face was covered in sweat, and a thin trickle of blood dribbled out of the corner of his mouth.

Jack didn't like Blunt, but he couldn't leave him behind.

"Come on!" Jack cried, shaking Blunt by the shoulder. But Blunt didn't move. Jack shook him again.

"Come on, we've got to get out of here!" he shouted.

Blunt blinked at him, then with incredible speed he lashed out and grasped Jack's arm.

"It was all his idea!" he shouted, his breath rank on Jack's face. "He wants to be a bloody captain! That's what he wants!"

The words shot out of Blunt's mouth thick and fast. Jack could hardly breathe. "It was his idea! The bomb. It was his idea, not mine! He wanted to go back and rescue them, you see. He wanted to be the big hero. Then they'd have to promote him. But I didn't want there to be a bomb. I didn't want that!"

The words hit Jack like a hammer.

"It was *your* bomb!" he screamed. "It was *your* idea!"

With a tremendous crack a boulder fell from the crest of a mountain and rolled down into the jungle.

Jack pulled away from Blunt's grasp. "We've got to go! What's the matter with you?"

Fireballs rained through the trees and more rocks toppled from the mountains. The noise was deafening. The cliffs could collapse at any moment. Blunt gazed like a bewildered child at the jungle burning around them. Jack grabbed the mechanic's arm and struggled to drag him down the path toward the beach.

Another glowing river of lava snaked down the far side of the mountain and was already flowing into the lagoon. The water steamed and bubbled around it. On the other side of the bay, the *Hyperion* was preparing to leave. Black smoke poured from her funnel.

"She's going!" Jack shouted as he ran onto the sand.

Blunt suddenly recovered his senses, and pushing Jack out of the way, he charged toward the water's edge. He dived in and tried to swim to the ship, but within seconds he realized his terrible mistake—the water was boiling hot. Blunt tried to return to shore, but it was too late. His body rolled over in the water and bobbed away among the crashing rocks. Jack looked away.

When he looked up, he saw that the *Hyperion* was moving toward the opening in the rock. Jack stared at the ship. They were leaving him behind.

Then through the smoke and steam he saw Quixote cutting toward him in the skiff. The captain rowed hard, mindless of the fireballs falling into the water around him. He brought the skiff as close to the shore as he could.

"Hurry, get in!" he cried. "The water's so hot it's melting the tar on the boat. We don't have much time!"

Jack jumped into the skiff. As Quixote rowed toward the *Hyperion*, Jack could feel the boiling water eating into the bottom of the boat. Water seeped between the boards, and the soles of his shoes began to melt. The skiff was sinking fast.

When they reached the *Hyperion*, Beryl leaned over the rail and offered Jack her hand.

Jack held up the broken prop.

"You went back for that?" she asked. "That was really courageous."

"We can use it as a guide to make a new one for the *Betsy II*," Jack said. "That's if we ever get out of here. Take it, will you?"

But as Jack passed her the broken propeller, the wet wood slipped through his fingers.

"No!" he cried as he tried to catch it. He wasn't quick enough.

The propeller smacked Quixote in the face and would have fallen into the water, but Quixote deftly caught it in the crook of his arm.

"Now move!" he yelled in a voice like thunder.

Jack moved and only just in time, for as Quixote stepped out of the skiff and onto the ladder, the little boat sank beneath the bubbling green water.

Quixote dropped the broken propeller on the deck and ran to the wheel. "Quarter steam ahead!" he bellowed. "Take it slow, Eric. We want to get out in one piece. Thomas, to the prow! Dorothy, get inside out of the way. The rest of you—to the rails!"

"I'll do no such thing," muttered Dorothy as she hurried past Jack and took her position beside Horatio at the rail. "Get inside, indeed!"

The engines roared to life, and Quixote swung the ship around and headed for the hole in the rocks. As the ship disappeared into the dark corridor, half the mountain fell into the lagoon and sealed the tunnel behind them.

Inside the corridor they could hear the muffled sound of rock ripping apart. It was like being inside a giant's mouth when the giant was grinding his teeth. It was pitch-black and extremely hot. The men lit the lamps, and the order was given for each man to wait in the shrouds and watch the walls on either side. The ship slowed until they were only inching along. The captain kept a cool, steady hand on the wheel.

Then Horatio shouted, "The rocks! They're moving together. They'll squeeze the life out of us!"

Jack reached out and laid his hands flat on the wall. He could feel the rock move toward him and then sink back. It was hot to the touch and growing hotter. It moved in waves like a solid sea.

Soon they didn't need the lamps. The walls were starting to glow, and the entire ship was bathed in a dim orange light. The light came from lava on the other side of the rock as the mountain melted.

As the orange light grew brighter, Jack saw Thomas

Fell crawl onto the bowsprit to watch for the opening. At last it came.

"Hard to port, Captain! Now!" yelled Thomas.

The ship pulled around, and Quixote ordered full steam ahead. They tore through the mountain and at last shot out into the smoky daylight. Behind them, the rocks ran with lava.

They were out of the corridor, but still a long way from safety. The overhang was breaking up, and boulders as big as houses were crashing about the *Hyperion* like hailstones in a storm.

There was no time to circle the island using the channel in the reef. Quixote gave the order to load the forward cannons and fire at will into the sea. The men worked in teams to load, fire, and reload the guns as they blasted through the reef. Flying shards of coral joined the hail of rocks and fireballs as the reef exploded around them.

The reef broke up easily, and within minutes the *Hyperion,* her wooden sides stuck like a pincushion with slivers of the needle-sharp coral, was steaming through the newly made channel of clear water.

"Why didn't you do that to get to the island?" asked Jack as they headed toward the open sea. "Wouldn't that have been easier?"

"Maybe it would," replied Horatio with a smile. "But then Welkin Isle would have been crawling with all sorts of everyone looking for buried treasure and the like. Captain didn't want that. It was Dorothy's island. He knew she liked it nice and quiet."

As they broke through the final ring of the reef, the island erupted in a frenzy of fire and molten rock. Lava spewed from the shattered peak and ran like red-hot molasses into the sea. The reef exploded and the great cliffs collapsed until finally the island was nothing more than a bright, fiery lake of lava.

The disruption of the earth stirred up the sea, and the waters gathered together in an enormous wave, a great watery avalanche taking with it anything that lay in its path. The *Hyperion* was picked up along with rocks and debris and swept far away. When at last the wave wore itself out, Welkin Isle was no more than a faint red glow on the horizon.

Chapter 21

The Navigator

Once the *Hyperion* was sailing in calm waters the crew set about clearing away the debris that had fallen from the island. The decks were littered with shards of rock and coral, and every surface was coated in fine volcanic ash. The men were in good spirits as they worked. They laughed and congratulated themselves on their narrow escape. They called the *Hyperion* a miracle ship again and again.

Jack stayed out of everybody's way. He crouched at the foot of the foremast and stared at the sea as the ship rose and fell. What Blunt had told him kept creeping into his mind. Had it really been Gadfly's idea to destroy the *Belle?* It couldn't have been. Gadfly wouldn't have done that, would he? Jack didn't want to think about it, and yet he thought of little else.

Every man must make his own way in the world. It was

Gadfly's motto. But surely Gadfly wouldn't have gone so far as to set a bomb on the *Belle* to make his way in the world? Jack couldn't believe that. Blunt must have been lying.

But then an unpleasant picture of Gadfly's face flashed sharp and clear in his mind. It was the way Gadfly had looked when he'd hit Blunt with the butt of the gun; it was the way he'd looked when he'd talked about Beryl; it was the way he'd looked when Jack had discovered him on the cliff. Gadfly had said he'd removed the *Viper*'s radio, but he hadn't. Maybe he'd just forgotten. Gadfly wouldn't have lied to him. He wouldn't. Blunt had lied. Not Gadfly!

Jack rubbed his eyes with his fists and groaned. He stayed on his own, wrapped up in his thoughts, until the sun set. A cold, lonely moon rose high and scattered silver on the water.

That same moon is looking down on my father, he thought. *If only there was some way to find him, if only . . .*

"Jack?" Beryl called.

Jack roused himself and stood up.

"Dorothy wants to see you. Come on. And bring your sextant and the reading you took. Hurry—it's important."

Jack ran to get the sextant, then joined Beryl at the door of Quixote's cabin. Inside, they found Dorothy sitting at the desk. She looked up and smiled as they entered.

"Beryl told me all about your father and his airship," she said, pushing Nelly off her shoulder and straightening her hair. "If you let me have that sextant reading, I'll have a go at working out where they might have come down."

Jack's spirits rose. "You know how to navigate?" he said, lifting the notebook out of the case.

Dorothy smiled. "I do. I grew up on a ship. My father was a captain." She set the notebook on the table and copied down the reading. "Now pass me the almanac, would you?"

Jack's hopes fell. "It's no use," he said. "Quixote doesn't have an almanac, he told me so himself."

Dorothy frowned. "Well, what's that? Scotch mist?" she asked, pointing to the bookshelf behind Jack. Jack turned around and gasped when he saw the fat black book in the middle of the shelf. It was upside down, but it was clearly the almanac Quixote had said he didn't have. Jack pulled it down and handed it to Dorothy.

"Why would Captain Quixote say he didn't have one?" whispered Beryl almost to herself.

Jack shook his head. It seemed strange to him, too. Then he remembered Quixote's odd behavior when they'd taken the books from the *Lady Anne*. Suddenly he understood. "Unless," he whispered, "Quixote had no idea he had one."

"Pardon?" asked Beryl.

"Look!" Jack cried. He rushed around the desk, pulled open the drawer, and took out Quixote's journal. He opened it up and showed Beryl and Dorothy the big childish letters and drawings. "Ha! Of course!" Jack exclaimed. "Quixote didn't know he had an almanac because he doesn't know how to read!"

Beryl frowned. "There's nothing funny in not being able to read, Jack," she said, taking the journal from him and putting it back in the drawer. "At least he's trying to learn. He probably never had the chance to go to school like you."

Jack felt embarrassed then. He hadn't laughed because he thought it was funny, but because he'd been surprised.

"Ehem," Dorothy coughed, holding out her hand. "If you'll let me have the sextant, Jack, I'll find out exactly where we are now."

Jack handed it to her, and Dorothy stood up and hurried on deck to take a reading. When she returned, she jotted down the figures and consulted the almanac, then made a mark on the map.

"Now we know where we are," she said brightly. "Let's see if we can't find your father. What time did you take your reading, Jack?"

"I took it at"— Jack consulted the notebook in the sextant case—"at thirteen hundred hours and sixteen minutes. That's about one-fifteen in the afternoon, right?"

"Right," Dorothy said. She flipped the almanac to the proper day, found the time and the reading . . .

"There!" she said, making another mark on the map. "That's where you were when you took that reading. Now, you say the bomb was set to go off three hours later?"

Jack nodded. "I heard them say sixteen hundred hours. That's four o'clock."

"So," Dorothy said, "we know where the airship was just before you fell, and if it was locked on course and traveling at, let's say, this speed for almost three hours, I reckon they are about . . ."

Dorothy laid a ruler across the map and checked over her figures one last time. "If my calculations are correct, I'm quite certain that they came down somewhere about here." Dorothy drew a large *X* on the map.

Beryl was looking at the map over Dorothy's shoulder. "Based on where we are now and considering the miraculous nature of this ship," she said, "I'll bet we could be there in just two days."

Jack didn't need to hear any more. He started for the door. "Quixote will have to help us when he sees this! He can't refuse me now!"

"Jack, be careful," warned Dorothy. "He might be . . . er . . . sensitive about this."

Jack nodded. He would do nothing to embarrass the captain. Jack found Quixote leaning against the rail. The captain's eyes were far away, gazing at something that Jack could not see. A little smile lifted the corners of his mouth, and he was humming a tune that Beryl had been singing earlier.

Jack shuffled his feet and coughed. Quixote spun around, his face a fiery red. He drew his eyebrows together and frowned.

"What are you doing, sneaking up on me like that?" he demanded.

"I . . . er . . . Dorothy . . ."

"Spit it out!"

"Dorothy's a navigator," Jack said, "and, well, she found an almanac on your shelves. . . ."

At this, Quixote's face turned even redder. Jack stumbled on.

"Using the reading I took, she's found where my father's airship came down. We can be there in a day or two. . . ."

Quixote's eyes blazed with fury. He pinned Jack against the rail.

"How many times do I have to tell you? By the head of Gregor Ladislav Lavinovich, we are never going north!" Quixote thundered.

"But there are men dying. . . ."

"Don't you understand?" hissed Quixote. "There are eight men, two women, and one stubborn boy who will die as well if we try to rescue your father. We can never return to the Polar Sea. Never!" Quixote shoved Jack toward the galley. "Now go and help cook."

Jack glowered at the captain. "I'll rescue my father somehow," he vowed. "I'm not going to let him down."

Quixote turned away and stared out at the cold sea. "I believe that while you're on this ship you have work to do. I suggest you do it."

That supper in the forecastle Jack dished up stew, handed around the bread and butter, and gave out the mugs of tea, but he hardly noticed what he was doing. All the time he was thinking about Quixote. Why did he still refuse to return to the Polar Sea? Beryl and her airplane had proved that Jack's story was true. And with Dorothy's help, Jack had found his father's location. What else did Quixote want?

Then Jack remembered the look that had passed through Quixote's eyes at the campfire. Suddenly Jack knew what that look was. It was fear. Quixote was afraid!

Jack thumped the table, rattling the plates. The crew looked up.

"Why won't he go back to the Polar Sea?" Jack asked.

No one answered. The men exchanged glances, then all turned their eyes back to their food. Jack shook Sky's shoulder.

"Tell me why he doesn't dare go back there!" Jack insisted.

Sky pulled away and said nothing. Jack grabbed Thomas's arm, then Horatio's, then Smith's, but not one of them would meet his eyes. Not one of them would look at him.

"I'll ask him myself, then," Jack said.

Eric caught Jack by the wrist and held him fast. Jack tried to wriggle free.

"You can't ask him," Eric said. "And even if you did, he'd never tell you why."

"What is it he's afraid of?" insisted Jack.

"You know what," Eric said.

"It's why he curses that name," whispered Thomas.

"You mean Gregor Ladislav Lavinovich?" asked Sky.

"Aye, that's it." Thomas nodded. "It was him who built it."

"Quiet!" snapped Eric. "You've said too much already."

"You mean he's afraid of the *Nem*—" Jack began, but Eric twisted his wrist and Jack cried out in pain.

"He'll do what he said at the campfire," Eric said. "Understand that, boy. If you so much as whisper that name under your breath in the dead of night, you'll not wake to see the dawn."

Eric let him go, and Jack sprawled to the floor. The men returned to their suppers in silence. Jack rubbed his wrist and watched the men eat as though everything was all right. But everything wasn't all right. Jack stared at the floor. Between his feet he saw a small knothole. A dim beam of yellow light shone up through it. Jack knelt down. He could see the engineer's desk below. Suddenly Jack remembered the shipwright's blueprint he had seen on the engineer's desk on his first day on board the *Hyperion*. Wasn't it a plan of the *Nemesis?*

Jack hurried out of the forecastle. He had to find that blueprint!

The engineer was on deck with Beryl. They were measuring the *Betsy II* and discussing the best way to make a new propeller using the *Viper*'s broken one as a guide. Jack quietly sneaked past and slipped belowdecks.

In the engine room, a single lamp burned above the engineer's desk. Jack opened the top drawer. It was crammed full of stuff, but there was no plan. He pulled the drawer all the way out and tipped it over. Rubber bands, ink bottles, and pencil stubs fell onto the desk. Jack peered into the empty drawer. There was a small loop of ribbon stuck to the wood at the back of the drawer. He pulled it and the bottom of the drawer lifted up to reveal a shallow compartment. There was the plan.

Jack lifted it out and unfolded it across the desk. He gasped at the mass of pipes and cogs, the confusion of levers and cylinders, and the maze of boilers and tanks before him. The scale of the warship was incredible. The size of the engines, the height of the funnels, the thickness of the hull, were fantastic.

Jack heard someone cough behind him and spun around. It was the engineer.

"You're the one!" Jack whispered. "You're Gregor Ladislav Lavinovich, aren't you? You designed this. You designed the *Nemesis!*"

The engineer passed his hand over his face and nodded.

"Yes, to my shame, I did," he said. "And every day I regret it with all my heart. Look at her, Jack. What a monster! There are no cabins, no captain's quarters, no chart room. The *Nemesis* doesn't need them because she doesn't need a crew."

The engineer sat down and looked over the plans. He shook his head. "When I was young, I invented a sealed engine that would run for years without refueling or maintenance. When they heard about it, my government recruited me to work on a secret project. They wanted me to design an unmanned war machine. They told me it was the dawn of a new era, that soon no one would ever have to die for their country again."

The engineer removed his glasses and rubbed his eyes. "They told me they would share the technology of machine-against-machine warfare with every country in the world, so that soon there would be no young men on the battlefield, just machines. You see, that was how I thought it would be, but I was wrong.

"My only excuse is that I was very young. I was slow

to realize that my government had no intention of sharing the new technology, and while I sat in my laboratory and dreamed of a world in which young lives would not be wasted, they took my plans and built the *Nemesis*."

The engineer looked at Jack with pale, watery eyes. He leaned forward, and his voice shrank to a whisper.

"There was a small country which had been a thorn in my government's side for many years," the engineer said. "They sent the *Nemesis* to destroy it. They killed thousands of people, just to show that they could. I begged them to stop, but they wouldn't listen to me. I knew then that I was becoming a problem for them, and that if I wasn't quiet, they would find a way to silence me. So with the help of some friends I escaped from my country and lived in exile."

"What happened to the *Nemesis?*" asked Jack in a whisper.

The engineer sat back in his seat and passed his hand over the plans on the desk.

"Before the government had another chance to use it, the *Nemesis* broke out of their control. Exposure to electrical storms had affected her equipment, and she became a rogue warship, an uncontrollable killing machine. She sailed north and was trapped by the electrical storms that rage around the Arctic. So she roamed the waters of the Polar Sea sinking any vessel that dared to venture there. And she roams there still."

Jack was silent a moment. Then he asked, "But how did you end up here?"

The engineer shook his head. "Eventually everyone blamed me for all the deaths caused by the *Nemesis*. I knew it was true. Deep in despair, I boarded a ship, and when we were far from land, I threw myself and my suitcase full of plans into the water. It is ironic that Quixote, the man who curses my name, fished me out of the sea and saved my life."

He smiled and shrugged his shoulders. "It's more than twenty-five years since I designed the *Nemesis*, but I remember one thing very clearly. I designed her to be completely indestructible. Every day I look for a way to destroy her—hoping, praying that I made a mistake— but every day I fail to find one."

The engineer began to fold up the plan of the *Nemesis*.

"Shouldn't you tell Quixote about this?" Jack asked. "Maybe *he* could find a way to destroy your warship."

"If I tell Quixote who I am, he'll throw me overboard." The engineer shook his head and continued to fold the plan. "No, Jack, don't look at me like that. I don't care if I live or die, but without me, the *Nemesis* will go on forever. And I can't allow that. Before I die, I have to find a way to stop it."

Chapter 22

A New Shipmate

That night Jack dreamed that he was trapped on top of the airship's hull. Gadfly was there, and Blunt, too, and they were pushing him with long poles. He tried to keep his balance, but Gadfly caught him by the foot and flipped him up in the air.

As he fell toward the sea, the milky water turned grassy green. It wasn't the sea at all, it was a field, and there were people standing in it. Lots of people, and they were all happy to see him. At the center of the crowd his mother held a baby up to greet him.

He smiled at the baby. But then he saw that it wasn't a baby, it was a man wrapped up, swaddled against the cold. A man with icicles in his matted beard and white frost all over his face. It was his father. Jack cried for someone to come and help, but the crowd had changed. Now twenty frozen specters sat crouched around a dying fire in a white desert of ice.

Jack woke with a start to find Beryl standing over him.

"Gadfly did it," Jack said. "Gadfly put the bomb on the *Belle.*"

Beryl touched Jack's hair. "I'm sorry, Jack," she said. "Speaking of that weasel, I think you'd better come and take a look outside."

On deck everyone was leaning over the rail and jeering down at the water.

Jack hurried to the rail and looked down. Lying in the water was a half-submerged yellow plane.

"What are you waiting for?" screamed Gadfly, clinging to the wreckage of the *Viper.* "Get me out of here! I'm going to freeze!"

"Jack, can you see the propeller?" asked Beryl. "Can you see it?"

Jack understood what she meant. If the propeller was there, they could salvage it for the *Betsy II.* The *Viper* bobbed around in the water and turned its nose toward the ship. There was no propeller.

"I never tightened the nuts," said Jack. "That's probably what brought him down."

A wave crashed over the *Viper,* filling her cockpit to the brim. She sank in seconds, a yellow bird disappearing beneath the water.

"Help!" cried Gadfly weakly.

"You can't leave him there," Dorothy insisted. "Get him out."

Gadfly floated farther from the ship and disappeared behind a wave. When the wave rolled away, there was no sign of him.

"There he is," yelled Sky from the rigging, pointing to where Gadfly struggled against a wave a hundred feet away.

"Let's pick him up," Quixote said. "Fine on the port bow, Mr. Lamb!"

A few minutes later Quixote threw a rope to Gadfly, and the pilot was pulled aboard.

"Jack?" Gadfly whispered hoarsely. Then he closed his eyes and collapsed onto the deck.

"Take him below and get him dried off," Quixote ordered.

"I don't like it. He's another Jonah!" whined Horatio as Eric and Sky pulled Gadfly to his feet. "He'll bring us more bad luck."

"He will," agreed Smith. "He makes thirteen on board if you count the monkey. That's got to be unlucky."

Jack didn't like it, either. He could hardly bring himself to look at Gadfly.

"Jack . . . ," said Beryl softly.

But Jack didn't want to talk to her. He shook his head and ran below. Jack worked hard in the galley all afternoon. He scrubbed and polished and cleaned, and by the end of the day it was a different room. But thoughts of Gadfly's treachery still crept into Jack's head. He'd almost finished cleaning under the stove when he heard someone calling his name through the grating in the bottom of the wall.

"Jack, is that you?" whispered the voice.

It was Gadfly. He was being held in the little pantry next to the galley. Jack scuttled out from beneath the stove and stood up.

"Jack, can you hear me?" Gadfly asked again.

Jack rattled the pots in the sink.

"Come on, Jack, I know you're angry. You have every right to be, but put that aside. Won't you speak to me, Jack? Jack?"

Jack didn't answer.

"Jack, come on. It's me!"

Jack turned to leave the galley, but as he reached the steps Gadfly said, "Jack, you have to hear me out. I'm the only chance your father's got."

Jack wheeled around and threw open the door to the pantry.

"How can you say that?" he cried. But he stopped when he saw Gadfly. The lieutenant looked awful. His eyes were bloodshot and ringed with purple bruises.

"How can you say that?" Jack whispered.

"Because it's true," Gadfly said. He smiled at him. It

was the old friendly smile, but this time, Jack didn't buy it.

"I know what you did," Jack said. "Blunt told me. It's your fault they're lost; it's your fault they're dying. It's all your fault."

Gadfly's eyes flickered, but his mouth never lost its smile.

"Jack, Jack, it doesn't matter whose fault it was. What's important is that we find your father soon. When Beryl's plane is ready, we could take it and . . ."

"No," Jack said quietly as he backed out of the room. "No, we couldn't."

"Jack, it's the only way to help your father!"

But Jack closed the door and ran out onto the deck.

Chapter 23

Another Game of Challenges

Jack sat and brooded by the foot of the foremast. It seemed as though years had passed since the day of the *Belle*'s launch. If only he could go back; if only he could make it all different.

A piercing whistle brought his attention back to the ship. It was the signal for all hands on deck, but he didn't move.

When all was quiet, Jack heard Quixote shout, "It's a fine day, and we've nothing else to do. Who's for a game of challenges?"

The crew cheered, then huddled together and started muttering. Even Dorothy joined in their whispers. Beryl looked up from her work and watched them.

"Come on, what do you want me to do?" laughed

Quixote, rubbing his hands together. "Climb the mainmast blindfolded?"

"You'll have to wait," Dorothy said. "We're collaborating."

"We don't want to make it too easy for you this time," added Eric Lamb.

"Well, be quick about it," laughed Quixote.

Jack stood up and stared back along the ship. His eyes fell on Beryl's propellerless plane, sad and useless on the deck. Turning to the rail, he stared down at the deep green water. Every second they traveled farther and farther away from the Polar Sea. Jack lifted his head and stared at the empty ocean. Hadn't Quixote said that the Polar Sea was a vast place? If it was so big perhaps they could sail there, rescue his father, and leave without ever meeting the warship that Quixote feared so much. Wasn't there at least a chance of that? But even if there was, how could he persuade Quixote to take it?

Quixote leaped onto the ratlines. "Come on, stop dillydallying," he shouted. "Give me a proper challenge."

A proper challenge? Jack walked to the top of the companionway and stared across at Quixote.

"Come on, will you?" demanded the captain as he swung gracefully back down to the deck. "At this rate I'll be old before you've made up your minds."

Jack narrowed his eyes. A proper challenge? He stuck

his hands deep in his pockets and found the three rough rubies that he'd picked up on Welkin Isle. He pulled them out and then looked at Quixote.

"I have a challenge for you," he said. His voice sounded loud and high in his ears.

The smile fell from the captain's lips, and the huddle of men fell silent.

"Let's hear it, then," said Quixote.

Jack steeled himself. "I challenge you to save my father!"

"Pah!" said Quixote, waving him away.

Jack jumped onto the main deck and pushed his way through the men. He held the three rubies out to the captain.

"You said you didn't believe my story," Jack said, "but then Beryl came and proved it was true. You said we wouldn't be able to find the *Belle*, but then Dorothy worked out where she is. And yet you still refuse to help my father."

Quixote's frown deepened, but Jack went on. "I have a proper challenge for the great Quixote. I challenge you to face your fear—go back to the Polar Sea, find my father, and face the *Nemesis!*"

The crew drew back. Neither Jack nor Quixote moved. The captain's face grew dark. Everyone waited. On his honor, he could not refuse a serious challenge.

There was no movement on the ship. It seemed that

the very sea had stilled, as if the world was waiting for the reply.

Without a word, the captain slapped Jack's hand away. The three stones clattered to the deck. Quixote stormed into his cabin and slammed the door with an almighty bang. Jack was too stunned to move. Dorothy bent down and picked up the stones. The crew murmured among themselves.

"He's refused, he's not going to do it."

"Must be getting old."

"The boy went too far!"

Then the cabin door flew open, and Quixote came out holding Lard the cat by the scruff of the neck.

"What are you all—*achoo*—waiting for? Set the sails. Mr.—*achoo*—Lamb, head for the Polar Sea. There's a challenge to be met! And keep this blasted animal out of my way!" And with that he threw Lard into Jack's arms and disappeared back into his cabin, slamming the door behind him.

"Looks like you got what you wished for," said Dorothy as she handed the rubies to Jack. "Let's just hope we're not too late."

Jack turned to go, but Eric Lamb grabbed his arm and hissed in his ear. "You'd better start praying that this really is a miracle ship, lad, because we're going to need all the miracles we can get if we're going up against that iron monster."

Chapter 24

Zagraff

Jack was full of hope. With each passing minute they were a little closer to the Polar Sea. That they were also sailing closer to the *Nemesis* didn't bother him. He was not going to have his hopes dashed by thinking of the one thing that stood between him and his father.

The captain kept to his cabin for the rest of the day. He wouldn't see anyone, not even Dorothy. The air rang with his curses. Again and again he swore on the head of Gregor Ladislav Lavinovich, and Jack trembled for the engineer's safety.

With the engineer's permission, Jack told Beryl the true history of the *Nemesis*. Now the two of them pored over the plan of the warship while the engineer carved and smoothed and shaped a new propeller out of a piece of ship's planking. The day disappeared. Jack racked his brains to find a way to defeat the great iron ship or at least to avoid it once they reached the Polar Sea, but he could find nothing. It was very late when he folded his arms on the desk and fell asleep.

The engineer worked through the night, and Jack woke from his short uncomfortable sleep to the smell of varnish. Another coat of the slow-drying shellac and the propeller would be ready to try.

It was late morning when they heard Quixote's footsteps approaching. Quickly the engineer covered the desk in papers to hide the *Nemesis*'s plans.

No one had seen Quixote since Jack had challenged him. Now, as he entered the engine room with his head bowed and his face half hidden in shadow, he looked as though he had not slept for a month.

"I've thought and I've thought, but I can see no way through," he said to the engineer. He staggered to a post and clung to it. "It's a killing machine! It attacks anything, everything, that gets in its way. We escaped once because we were lucky. I don't think we will have such luck again."

Quixote's voice sank to a low growl. "To see that monstrous ship on the horizon is to know the coldest fear a man can know. It was made by a man who has no soul, a man with no conscience—that coldhearted villain, Gregor Ladislav Lavinovich. Blast him!"

The captain paused and wiped the sweat from his forehead.

"Isn't there a chance that it won't—" Jack began.

"Won't what?" Quixote snapped. "That it won't find us?" The captain shook his head. "The *Nemesis* will hunt us down the moment we sail into that sea.

"How can I face the *Nemesis* when I know it's certain death? I don't give a hang about my own hide, but to lead my crew into such danger is unforgivable. Isn't there anything we can do to save ourselves?"

The engineer shook his head. "The only way to save the *Hyperion* is to turn around and forget about going to the Polar Sea."

"No! I cannot," replied Quixote. "I've given my word, and I've accepted the challenge. If only I knew of some weakness in the iron belly of that monster, some chink in the armor. If only . . ." Quixote stopped. Something on the desk had caught his eye. "Am I going mad?" he whispered to himself. "I see it everywhere . . . everywhere." He took a step toward the desk.

Quixote was staring at a water glass on the desk. What had he seen there? Jack craned his neck and saw the top of a funnel and the letter *N* refracted through the wet bottom of the glass.

Gently Quixote lifted the glass. He paused and then fiercely pushed the papers off the desk.

"No!" he muttered as he stared down at the plan of the *Nemesis,* his chest heaving like the sea.

"Where did you get this?" he asked in a hoarse whisper, pointing a shaking finger at the plan. The engineer stood up. "Where did you get this?" Quixote asked again.

Beryl pulled Jack out of the way. "I'll get Dorothy," she said, and then she disappeared into the shadows. Quixote glared at the engineer.

"Speak, damn you," he warned, taking a step closer to the engineer. He towered over him. "How did you come by this?"

The engineer's hands trembled, but he answered Quixote bravely. "I drew it. The *Nemesis* is my design," he said. "I am Gregor Ladislav Lavinovich."

"No!" whispered Quixote as the blood drained from his cheeks. "On my ship? All this time you've been here on my ship?"

"It's . . . it's . . . not how you think," stammered the engineer.

"*Then tell me how it is before I kill you!*" Quixote thundered, grabbing the engineer by the throat. The engineer struggled and gasped for breath, but the captain held him tight.

"*Speak, damn you!*" screamed the captain as he dragged the engineer from his desk.

"He can't speak, you're squeezing the life out of him!" cried Jack as he tried to pull Quixote off.

"Quixote, stop that!" Dorothy commanded as she rushed into the room. "He's not an animal and neither are you. Let the man tell his story. Let him go!"

Quixote glared at her, then lifted the engineer by the collar and threw him against the desk.

"All right, tell it!"

Eric Lamb and the rest of the crew had heard the commotion and were gathered around the engine room door. They listened as the engineer told his story, much as he had told it to Jack. When he'd finished, he hung his head. "Now do with me what you will," he said.

Quixote slumped onto a stool and stared at the floor. It was as if all the fight had been knocked out of him.

"Zagraff," he said quietly. "The name of the country the *Nemesis* destroyed was Zagraff."

"How did you know that?" asked the engineer.

"I was born there," Quixote said. The engineer opened his mouth, but Quixote raised his hand.

"I was a boy of eleven when I came aboard this ship. I was a raw lad and ready for adventure. I left my mother and father and told them I'd be back in a year or two. But each time I thought to return there was always some new adventure that seemed more important. I always thought that I could go home anytime.

"Ten years passed before I saw my homeland again. As we sailed toward her, the land looked so green and fresh, the city shone pink and white, and the sight of it filled my heart with joy. My shipmates went ashore, and I was left on board as the solitary watch. I remember the day was so bright that I had to shield my eyes, but midway through my watch a shadow fell across the ship; it grew and crossed onto the land. I watched it as one watches the shadow of a cloud race across the fields. I waited for the sun to shine once more. But the day grew darker. I turned to see what sort of monstrous fog this was that could blot out the sun and turn the day to night. And that was when I saw the gleaming black hull of the warship. Before I could cry out, the iron devil fired its guns into the sleepy afternoon city. I watched as the monster destroyed the home I had dreamed of for so many years.

"The guns roared long into the night. When they finally stopped, the warship slid back into the fog that spewed from its funnels. Its guns rolled in their turrets like unblinking eyes seeking an enemy, though there was nothing but a funeral pyre. I watched as that evil warship vanished over the sea.

"I could not bear that I had been spared on board the *Hyperion*. I did not think of her as a miracle ship then, but only as some cursed barge on which I was doomed to sail, remembering forever that awful day. How I begged heaven that the warship would return and blast me and the *Hyperion* out of the water, but I was not so blessed. Instead, I was left to watch my home burn to ashes.

"After three days nothing remained. My family, my home, and my shipmates were gone, and, though I had not a scratch on my body, a knife had pierced my soul. I vowed that I would sail the seas and never once put into port until I found the . . ." Quixote closed his eyes. ". . . until I found the *Nemesis* and destroyed her."

He looked long and hard at the engineer, then finally he said, "I believe you when you say you were taken in by the politicians' lies. I have known you for twenty-five years, and I believe you to be a good man. I believe you are telling the truth."

He dropped his head in his hands and stared down at the floor. Curious expressions flickered across his face. Jack felt his heart fill with pity. How awful to have lost everything in one terrible afternoon to that invincible monster. And now Jack felt ashamed that he had goaded him into facing it again.

"I never found the *Nemesis* until two weeks ago," Quixote continued. He jerked his chin at the engineer. "You were so free with your advice. You always steered us clear of the northern waters, did you not? Was that because you knew?"

The engineer nodded. "It was common knowledge in the world that the *Nemesis* roamed the Polar Sea. You never told me, but I guessed what you were seeking although I did not know why. I thought it best to keep you away from there as long as possible."

Quixote nodded. "Finally I grew impatient and demanded that we search the icy waters. And there we found what I had searched for for so long." Quixote paused and rubbed his forehead. "When the *Hyperion* grazed her timbers on the flanks of that colossal hull, I knew my cause was lost and that my vow was useless. We cannot fight the *Nemesis,* I know now. I know it here." He tapped his chest above his heart and fell silent.

Jack jumped up. "But there must be a way to stop it," he said. "The *Nemesis* is just a machine."

The engineer shook his head. "The only way the *Nemesis* would stop is if some foreign matter got into the engine. That would upset the carefully balanced mechanics and the ship would . . ." He made a gesture with his hands, *boom!* "But the hull is a completely sealed unit. Nothing can get in there. I designed it that way. There are no doors or portholes. There was no need for them."

Jack shook his head. He hadn't come this far to give up now. He wasn't going to let some rogue warship, no matter how powerful, prevent him from getting to his father. There had to be a way.

"What about here?" asked Beryl, pointing to where the massive anchor chains hung out of the hull. "That seems more accessible. Why not try to get someone up there?"

"No use," replied the engineer. "That was seen as a weak point, so there is no connection between the chain locker and the rest of the ship."

Jack glanced around the engine room. His eye fell on the newly carved propeller.

"Wait a minute!" Jack said, running his finger along the plan. "When did you say the ship was built?"

"Twenty-six years ago," the engineer said. "Why?"

"Don't you see?" said Jack. "You didn't design it to fire in the air. The guns can't fire at planes. Look! We can attack from the air, and it can't fire at us."

The engineer shook his head. "The *Nemesis*'s deck has twenty-four inches of armor plating. You may be able to get past the guns, but you can't do anything once you're up there."

"Couldn't we do something—?" Beryl said. "I don't know . . . Drop a bomb down a funnel?"

"The funnels just lead to the furnaces," answered the engineer. "Anything you dropped down there would be eaten up by the flames. That's why there was no need to cover the funnels; any dirt or debris that got in there would simply burn up."

Jack ran his eyes over the plan; the six massive engines with their innumerable pistons and valves, the seven enormous funnels, each one bearing a letter of the hateful name—NEMESIS.

"*Nemesis,*" he whispered. Seven horrible letters that kept him from his father. "*NEM-E-SIS.*" Seven letters, seven funnels; seven funnels, six engines. He looked again at the six massive engines with their furnaces. Seven funnels—six engines.

"It doesn't make any sense," Jack said. "Why are there

seven funnels and only six engines? Why is there nothing below the middle funnel?"

The engineer glanced at the plan. "I designed it with six engines, but because they wanted to have the name *Nemesis* on the funnels, one funnel—the fourth—is a dummy. It's just there for balance. There's nothing below it. I left it blank and assumed that they would run the armored deck beneath . . . *Oh!*" he cried. "You don't suppose they—? No, they couldn't have. What if they did?" The engineer grabbed Jack by the shoulders. "*What if they did?* If they did, we can . . ." He pushed his glasses to the top of his head, then ruffled frantically through the pages of a scruffy red notebook and made several hurried calculations in the margins.

Jack could hardly breathe.

The engineer closed the book and sat back in his chair. "It is possible," he said, "that the plan was incomplete when they built the ship. There is no furnace beneath the fourth funnel; this may simply be a tube leading directly to the engines. If anything were dropped down there—a bomb, a spanner, a nail, anything—it would fall right into the workings of the engines. I designed these engines to run forever, but if some foreign body fell in there, the *Nemesis* would cease to function."

"I don't understand," said Beryl. "Why would they leave this open?"

"Because they followed my plans to the letter."

"But why did *you* leave it open?"

The engineer shrugged. "It was one of those things I was going to go back and fix later. You have to understand, I was the chief designer. I was rushed off my feet."

Quixote nodded. "But what if someone else dealt with it?"

"That's a risk we'll have to take," the engineer said. "But I rather think they were in such a hurry to try out their new weapon that they may have overlooked such a seemingly cosmetic problem. All we have to do is make a bomb of some sort and throw it down that funnel. The bomb will be easy enough to make, just a parcel of glue and nails that would . . ."

"Gum up the works?" suggested Jack.

"Exactly!" said the engineer.

Chapter 25

The *Nemesis*

With Dorothy navigating they reached the Polar Sea in just two days. They had entered the world of the midnight sun; there would be no stars that night. The first icebergs appeared on the horizon like undiscovered islands, and soon the sea was crowded with them. It took all of Eric Lamb's skill to steer the *Hyperion* safely through.

Jack helped Beryl fit the new propeller onto the *Betsy II*. Beryl screwed down the eight nuts the engineer had made and spun the blade. The engine roared to life. Beryl smiled at Jack. It looked as though the new propeller would work, but the true test would come when they tried to fly.

The engineer mixed nails, nuts, and bolts together in a thick fish-bone glue. Then he filled a small sack with the mixture and tied it with string. As long as Jack dropped it down the right funnel, this "bomb" would destroy the *Nemesis*.

That night Jack sat wrapped in his greatcoat and anxiously watched the sea. Beryl's radio had been silent for a day and a half, but that probably just meant that the *Belle*'s radio had run out of power. It didn't necessarily mean . . .

Doubts gripped Jack's mind. What if they were too late? He hugged his knees and tried to picture his father's face, but he couldn't remember what he looked like. Was this a sign? Did it mean that he should give up his search? Jack shook his head and pressed his fists against his forehead.

"No, he's still alive," he whispered. "I'd know it if he wasn't. I'd know it in my heart."

He turned and watched the crew. They were men just like the men on the *Belle*. He knew his challenge to Quixote had put all of them at risk, but there was no going back now. They had to go on.

The sea was caked with ice, and the *Hyperion* cracked and crunched through it, leaving a dark clear wake. It was so cold that Jack could feel his spit crackle when he opened his mouth, and the glare from the ice made his eyes sting. Nevertheless, he kept his eyes peeled for any sign of the downed airship.

When Dorothy came on deck to take a reading, Jack noticed Nelson peeking out from the front of her pea jacket. The monkey was shivering and his teeth were chattering. Dorothy tutted when she saw Jack staring at the ice.

"You'll ruin your eyes," she cautioned him.

"How much farther do you think?" he asked.

"If my calculations are correct, we can't be too far from where they came down."

Together they stared out into the whiteness until the ice on the sea became too thick for the *Hyperion* to break through. The hull began to creak and groan as the ice pressed in on all sides.

"We can't go any farther, Jack," said Quixote. "The ship'll break up if we try. We have to turn back."

"But we have to keep looking!" Jack insisted. "They could be just beyond that snowdrift."

"Jack, that snowdrift is tiny. Look!" Quixote threw a rough sapphire at the drift. It covered half of it. "You've got whiteout from staring at the ice too long. You can't tell the scale of anything anymore. We have to leave now. Listen to the ship. She'll crack like a walnut if we don't go soon."

Jack knew Quixote was right, but to give up now when they'd come so far, when they were so close . . .

"It's time to leave and save the ship," said Quixote, gently pulling Jack away from the rail. "Half steam astern," he called to Eric Lamb at the wheel.

"Aye, Captain," replied Eric.

The ship slowed, came to a stop, and then reversed out through the channel that they had carved in the ice, but just as they were about to turn, an almighty blast rocked the ship. Jack was sent careening across the deck. Above them the white sky exploded with fire.

The whole ship was thrown into chaos. The crew tumbled about the deck, clutching at anything that would keep them from falling into the freezing water.

A second explosion followed hard on the first. Sky clung to the top of the mainmast with his fingernails; as soon as the ship steadied itself, he scampered down like an elongated monkey.

Jack held tight to a lifeline and stared up into the sky. A shadow as deep and as dark as night stole across the ship. Jack shivered with fear. "The *Nemesis*," he whispered to himself. *"THE NEMESIS!"* he shouted.

Everyone watched in silence as the warship charged through the ice toward them. Puffs of smoke erupted from twenty or more of the *Nemesis*'s guns.

"Hold fast!" screamed Quixote as the shells exploded all around them. "We've got to get out of here!" he yelled. "Everyone to their posts now! We'll have to blast our way out of the ice. Hurry! Hurry!"

Beryl pulled Jack to his feet. "Come on! We've got to get the *Betsy II* into the water before the ship gets under way. It's up to us, Jack. The only way to defeat that monster is from above. Come on!"

The men helped Beryl and Jack winch the plane into the water. It was halfway down when a shell exploded less than a hundred yards in front of the *Hyperion*. Shards of ice flew out in all directions. A white boulder narrowly missed the *Betsy II*, but it smashed into the *Hyperion*'s mizzenmast, cracking it in two like a twig.

As Jack climbed into the plane, the engineer handed him the makeshift bomb.

"Remember, it's got to be the fourth funnel," he reminded Jack. "Miss, and we're lost. Good luck."

Once the *Betsy II* was on the water Jack ran to the foremost tip of the float and grabbed the propeller. He tried to pull it around with all his might, but it wouldn't budge. It had seized up with the cold. He tried again. This time he managed to move it, but not enough to start the engine.

"Come on, Jack! Hurry!" cried Beryl.

Jack put both hands on the upper blade of the propeller and breathed out as he swung it down in a wide sweeping arc.

"There she goes," yelled Beryl as the engine kicked into life. "Sweet as a button, isn't she? Come on, we've got work to do."

Jack scrambled onto the wing and climbed into the rear cockpit. He fastened the safety strap and looked at the control panel in front of him. It was exactly the same as the one in the *Viper*. The one he'd once been allowed to fly.

Quixote leaned out over the ship's rail. "Take care, both of you," he called, but his eyes were on Beryl as he spoke.

Beryl smiled at him and saluted, then she pulled her goggles over her eyes and set off.

She steered the *Betsy II* along the dark channel that the *Hyperion* had cut in the ice, heading directly toward the *Nemesis*. Shells exploded all around them. Jack blocked his ears. The water was already beginning to ice over, and the *Betsy II*'s floats crunched along the surface of the sea.

They were a quarter of a mile from the *Nemesis* when the new propeller began to stick. Beryl gave it more throttle, but there was obviously something wrong. The propeller whirred for a moment, stopped, then started again. If it did that when they were flying, they'd have no chance.

The *Nemesis* loomed ahead of them. If they didn't take off soon, they wouldn't have enough clear water. Beryl leaned forward in her seat and reached over the small windshield.

"Time for some superior engineering skills," she shouted, thumping twice on the plane's nose. The propeller sputtered and stalled once more, then roared into life. This time it didn't falter. They sped toward the *Nemesis* and took off in an almost vertical climb right in front of the gigantic bow. The mighty guns began to fire on the little plane. Beryl skillfully dodged the missiles.

Jack clung to the bomb in his lap and stared up at the great hull as it passed before them. As they rose, something rolled back from beneath Beryl's seat and knocked into his foot. It was a half-full flagon of Mr. Treacle's syrup. Jack looked back at the sea so far beneath them, then up at the enormous hull. It seemed to take forever to climb even as far as the first line of guns.

With the *Betsy II* gone, the *Hyperion* tried to outrun the *Nemesis*. But they were icebound on three sides, and their escape route was blocked by the approaching warship.

"There's a break to port," Sky hollered from the shrouds.

Quixote climbed up behind him and saw that the ice on the port side was no more than a narrow isthmus of thirty or forty feet. Beyond it there was a thin channel of clear water. If they could break through the ice, they could make a run for it. Quixote took the wheel, and the *Hyperion* began to turn.

"Half steam ahead!" commanded Quixote, and the ship nosed forward. Shells from the *Nemesis* burst all around them; one landed a few yards off the bow and smashed the ice in front of them. This was what the captain had been hoping for. He called for full steam ahead, and the *Hyperion* charged through the broken ice.

High above them the *Betsy II* rose into the sky.

The *Nemesis* suddenly stopped firing on the ship and turned all its attention to the little plane. The great ship raised its guns, training them on the *Betsy II*. Jack had guessed correctly—the guns could not be raised above a certain point—but the *Nemesis* fired before the *Betsy II* could get there. Two mighty blasts spun the plane through the air like a bug in a storm. Beryl struggled with the controls, but each time she began to climb, the *Nemesis* fired again, creating a barrage that prevented the *Betsy II* from flying any higher.

Meanwhile, on the sea below, the *Hyperion* had finally reached clear water. Quixote watched the great warship firing at the little plane. Suddenly all the anger Quixote had felt as he watched Zagraff burn and during all the long years of searching erupted inside him. It was time to stop looking for ways to escape. It was time to face the *Nemesis*.

"Turn her around!" he commanded. "Let's play David to her Goliath."

"Aye, Captain," replied Eric as he spun the wheel.

The *Hyperion* turned and scudded across the sea, smashing its way through the shattered ice, heading straight for the lethal cleaver bow of the invincible warship.

Quixote's fury spread about the ship until every man on board screamed and yelled as they raced toward the *Nemesis*. The *Hyperion* fired, and just for a moment the

Nemesis lowered its great foreguns. But it took only a moment for Beryl to fly above the line of fire. All at once the sky was filled with the sound of metal hitting metal as the guns clanged in frustration against the tops of the iron turrets. The *Betsy II* was now above the mighty warship, and the guns could not reach her.

Beryl half turned to Jack. "Pull your scarf over your face and get ready—I'm going down!" She rolled the *Betsy II* to the left and brought her in a wide circle around the enormous cloud of vile black smoke that pumped out of the *Nemesis*'s funnels.

"The fourth funnel," Jack said to himself as he clutched the parcel of glue and nails.

Then they plunged deep into the darkness.

Chapter 26

The Fourth Funnel

It was so dark inside the cloud of smoke that Jack worried he might not be able to see the funnels, but his worry vanished as the first funnel rose out of the gloom. Beryl flew wide of it to avoid the thick plume of smoke that poured from its mouth.

"One!" counted Jack. In the distance he could hear the pounding of the *Nemesis*'s guns. He briefly wondered how the *Hyperion* was faring.

"Two," he murmured as the second funnel loomed out of the darkness. What if the *Hyperion* had been hit? How would they rescue his father? Then he remembered. They weren't going to rescue his father. They'd been about to turn back when the *Nemesis* had found them.

"Three," he said, only half aware of the third funnel. They'd given up. He'd given up. Jack felt wretched.

Beryl brought the plane up and flew over the smokeless mouth of the fourth funnel.

"Four," Jack murmured to himself.

"Four!" Cursing himself for not paying attention, Jack leaned over the side of the plane and threw the bomb down toward the funnel.

For a moment it looked as though the bomb would go in. It caught against the rim of the funnel, teetered on the edge, and then toppled the wrong way, dropping down the outside of the funnel to the impregnable deck. Jack felt numb as Beryl pulled the *Betsy II* up out of the smoke.

Once they were in the clear air, Beryl half turned and stuck her thumb in the air. Jack shook his head.

"I missed!" he yelled above the noise of the engine.

"What?" Beryl almost lost control of the plane.

As Beryl rolled the *Betsy II* to the left, the flagon of syrup knocked against Jack's leg. Far below, he could see the *Hyperion* struggling against the *Nemesis*. Quixote's miracle ship was suffering under the relentless blows of the monstrous ironclad. It would take more than a miracle to survive the attack. The *Hyperion* cut quickly through the ice-strewn waters, zipping forward and then doubling back, and all the while firing on the great warship. Jack shook his head. He'd done everything wrong. He had failed his father and now he'd failed Quixote, too. Angrily he kicked the flagon with his foot.

Suddenly he had an idea. If all that was needed was something to gum up the works, then perhaps there was another way.

He tapped Beryl on the shoulder and held up the flagon.

"Let's try again!" he shouted.

Beryl nodded, pulled her scarf over her nose, and rolled the *Betsy II* back toward the black cloud.

As they plunged through the smoke, Jack kept his mind on what he was doing. He counted the funnels . . . One . . . two . . . three, and by the time the fourth funnel loomed in sight, Jack was leaning over the side of the plane. He prayed that the gooey syrup would do the trick. As they passed over the mouth of the fourth funnel, he threw the flagon into the murky depths.

Jack sat back in his seat. He'd done it. Now there was nothing to do but wait and see what happened. Beryl pulled back on the joystick, and the plane climbed out of the smoke. As they soared into the brightness, Jack pulled off his sooty scarf and breathed in the sweet, fresh air.

Then he realized that the guns of the *Nemesis* had stopped firing.

Beryl flew high. She wanted to keep the *Betsy II* clear in case the *Nemesis* exploded. Below them Jack saw the *Hyperion* draw away as well.

But the warship didn't explode. She just stopped. The

wind blew away the thick black clouds of smoke, and the crackles of blue lightning on her radio masts fizzled out. Everything was silent. It was as though the snow and ice had swallowed every sound.

The crew of the *Hyperion* gazed at the warship looming above them. The *Nemesis,* though quiet, was still an awe-inspiring sight. Quixote's eyes burned with the tears he'd never shed for his parents and his country.

Suddenly a sound like the crack of a metal whip broke the silence and sent a shudder rippling along the length of the *Nemesis*'s hull. Then the air was filled with a terrible noise as the six massive engines shed every nut and bolt that had held them in place. The *Nemesis* was coming undone.

The funnels began to fall. The men on the *Hyperion* watched as the first funnel toppled into the second, and the second into the third, and so on until all seven funnels lay crumpled on the deck.

The engineer stood at the *Hyperion*'s rail and watched the prow of the *Nemesis* rise out of the sea. In his hand he clutched the plans of his unmanned warship. He watched the treacherous cleaver bow lift to the heavens, wavering above the *Hyperion* like an executioner's ax. The crew trembled. Everyone on board, save for the engineer, clung to the person closest to them. Dorothy grabbed Quixote, Mr. Treacle held on to both Lard and Sky, and Thomas quickly, and without thinking, turned and wrapped his arms about his brother, Horatio. The twins held each other tight.

Silently the *Nemesis* began to slip backward.

"She's going down!" the twins whispered at the same time. They turned to each other in amazement. Their silence had been broken, and neither of them had been the first to speak! They threw back their heads and laughed.

"She's going down!" they cried for all they were worth.

The engineer lifted the plans high above his head and threw them as far out into the water as he could.

"Never again," he vowed under his breath. "Never again!"

Quixote smiled and rested his hand on the engineer's shoulder as the *Nemesis* slipped down into the deep, deep sea.

But the *Nemesis* wasn't quite finished. She had her swan song yet to sing. It was a short song of just one note. With her prow pointing heavenward she fired one last shot into the sky, then sank forever beneath the black waters.

The warship's last shell exploded so close to the *Betsy II* that the tiny windshield flew off and struck Beryl on the head. Beryl slumped back in her seat, unconscious, as the plane spun out of control.

Chapter 27

The Mountain of Snow

"Beryl!" Jack cried as the *Betsy II* spun through the air. Jack saw a mad swirl of sky, then sea, then sky. He grabbed the joystick in front of him, but he didn't know which way was up. If he tried to climb and they were upside down, he could end up driving them into the sea all the faster. But if he didn't do something, they'd crash anyway.

Jack gritted his teeth, pulled back on the joystick, and gave her more power. The *Betsy II* screamed through the air and hurtled toward the black water. Jack's eyes smarted behind his goggles as he watched the hands on the altimeter spin crazily. He pulled back harder.

"Come on," he screamed. "Come on!"

Then, quite suddenly, just a few feet above the water, the plane responded. She pulled out of her dive. Her floats skimmed the dark sea, shooting up great arcs of spray. Jack cut back on the throttle and somehow managed to control the plane as she dipped down to the water again and again.

The *Hyperion* was ahead of him in the channel. There wasn't enough room to land. He would have to fly over the ship.

He pulled back on the joystick and the *Betsy II*'s nose began to rise, but as it did, the propeller started to cut out again. Jack tried to increase the power, but he only succeeded in narrowing the distance between the plane and the ship. The propeller stuck again.

He would have to try Beryl's method. He unfastened his safety belt and, trying to keep control of the plane by looping his foot around the joystick, he leaned over the front cockpit and thumped hard on the nose of the plane. Beryl groaned and rolled her head. Then, opening her eyes and seeing the *Hyperion*'s masts rushing toward them, she sat up and caught Jack full in the stomach. The blow knocked him out of the plane. Jack only just managed to catch hold of the rim of the cockpit as the propeller kicked in and the plane shot forward.

Fully conscious now, Beryl grabbed the controls and guided the plane into the air. Jack screwed his eyes shut and gritted his teeth, struggling to hold on. Beryl rubbed the bruise on her head as she brought the plane around. They flew low over the ice.

"Jack!" shouted Beryl, half turning in her seat. "Are you all ri—"

The sight of him hanging by his fingertips to the outside of the plane gave her such a shock that she pressed her foot down hard on the rudder bar, causing the plane to swing around so violently that Jack lost his grip and fell. Beryl tried to grab him, but it was too late.

"*Jack!*" she screamed as he tumbled toward the ice.

Everyone on the *Hyperion* watched him fall like a rag doll toward a mountainous snowdrift. But no one saw him land. No one could bear to watch that. They all turned their eyes away.

Quixote was the first to speak.

"Bring her in as close to the shore as you can, Eric. We'll go and pick him up."

Eric Lamb nodded and wiped his eyes on his shoulder.

Beryl landed the *Betsy II* on the water and taxied to the edge of the ice. She climbed out of the plane and ran across the snow.

"Jack, are you all right? Can you hear me?" Beryl shouted as she ran toward the hill.

Jack was sprawled across the soft snow on the top of the snowdrift. He waved weakly and tried to sit up, but the snow beneath him moved.

"Hang on, Jack," Beryl called. "I'll come and help you down." She tried to climb up the snowdrift, but she couldn't get a toehold, and every time she tried, she slid back to the ground.

"Oh!" she groaned, and as she kicked the hillside in frustration, a large cake of snow slid down on top of her. Beryl shook it off and pulled her goggles from her eyes.

Something glinted in front of her. Beryl reached out and picked some of the frozen snow away to reveal a small patch of silvery gray canvas. She pressed it, and the canvas sank inward beneath her hand. When she let go, the hillside quivered.

"Well, I'll be!" she said. Quickly she began to prize the snow away with her fingers, but it was frozen hard and difficult to remove. So she hit and kicked it until a small avalanche of snow fell down and almost buried her.

"Whaaaaa!" cried Jack as the falling snow carried him away. He rode the avalanche and landed in a heap on the ground. He groaned as Beryl pulled him to his feet.

"Jack, look!" cried Beryl, shaking him. "You've found her! You've found the *Belle!*"

Jack just looked at her with his mouth open. His arm ached horribly and he didn't know why Beryl was shouting at him, or why her face was lit up with excitement.

"Look," she cried. She began to hit and kick at the snow. Then all at once a large piece of snow fell away, revealing an enormous letter. It was a *B* as big as a house.

"It's the *Belle!*" he gasped.

Jack gazed at the *Belle* and smiled. But suddenly the

smile fell from his face. They'd found the *Belle,* but where was his father?

Holding his injured arm, Jack ran along the side of the airship.

"Jack, wait," Beryl shouted as she ran after him.

As Eric Lamb brought the *Hyperion* alongside the ice, everyone on board was watching Jack and Beryl. No one noticed Gadfly as he stole away from the ship and ran across the ice toward the *Betsy II.*

Jack stumbled in the snow and the pain in his arm shot up into his shoulder, but he kept on running. At the far end of the airship the tail fin rose into the sky like a snow-covered tower. Jack's lungs burned with the cold air. There was no sign of anybody anywhere.

Then Jack saw the nine snow-covered graves that lay in the shadow of the *Belle.* Each neat white hump had a small cross made of broken airship girders at its head. Jack stopped and listened to the wind blowing through the canvas. He felt lonelier than he had ever felt before.

Every man must make his own way in the world. Gadfly's motto echoed in his thoughts. Jack shook his head. The words themselves weren't wrong, but the way Gadfly had used them was. Gadfly didn't care if other people suffered just as long as he got what he wanted. That was Gadfly through and through. And what about Quixote? Jack realized now that no matter how harsh Quixote seemed, at heart he thought only of the good of his crew. He was very like Jack's father in that way.

"Oh!" cried Jack at the thought of his father. "Oh, please, be alive, please."

"Jack!" cried Beryl. Jack looked up.

Gadfly was running toward the *Betsy II*. He was trying to get away. Quixote and the others were running after him, but they were a long way behind.

"No!" Jack screamed. He couldn't let Gadfly get away. Not after what he'd done.

Beryl and Jack charged across the ice after Gadfly. Beryl was closer and soon caught Gadfly's sleeve. She hung on and tried to slow him down.

"Get to the plane, Jack!" she cried. "Move it out of his reach!"

Jack ran on toward the plane. Gadfly spun around and his fist caught Beryl in the stomach. Winded, she fell to her knees.

Jack looked back and saw Gadfly racing toward him. Jack turned and ran, willing his legs to move faster than they'd ever moved. He had never outrun Gadfly before, but this time he had to.

Somehow he reached the plane first and, with one arm, swung the propeller into action. The engine roared to life. He looked back. Gadfly was less than twenty yards away. Jack scrambled onto the wing and into the cockpit. He was backing the plane away from the ice when Gadfly leaped on the wing and grabbed him by the shoulders.

"Thanks for getting her started, Jack," he laughed as he yanked Jack out of the cockpit and pushed him off the plane. Jack landed hard on the ice. The pain in his arm was excruciating. He lay on his belly, unable to get up.

As Gadfly climbed into the cockpit, the propeller started to sputter and slow. "Damn!" hissed Gadfly, half lifting himself out of his seat.

Jack could just make out Quixote and the crew running across the ice, but they were still too far away to help. Then Jack heard other footsteps thundering close by. He tried to turn toward the airship, but as he did, something large leaped over him. Jack craned his neck and looked toward the plane. Gadfly's face was full of terror. Some sort of snow-covered creature, big and white like a polar bear, pulled him out of the plane and threw him across the ice. Gadfly screamed.

Jack heard Quixote and his crew run up behind him. They caught Gadfly as he tried to get up off the ice. "That's it, lads, hold him fast," cried Quixote.

Jack looked up and saw the creature bending over him. It knelt down and pawed his cheek gently with its huge snowy hand.

"Jack? Is it really you?" it asked.

Beneath the icicles and the snow-blistered face, Jack's father's eyes smiled down at him.

Chapter 28

The Voyage Home

The thirty-four survivors of the airship crash had almost given up hope of ever being rescued, but when they saw the *Hyperion* waiting by the ice, they knew that they were really going home. A few of them were strong enough to walk to the ship, but many had to be carried on stretchers.

Thomas and Horatio sang softly as they carried the men to the ship and laid them gently on the deck. The twins worked well together. It was as though there had never been any rift between them.

Dorothy supervised the care of the survivors on board the ship. All of them had terrible frostbite, and she knew that it was important not to make them warm too quickly. With Sky as her helper and Nelson on her shoulder, she tried to make each man as comfortable as possible. She also tended to Jack's arm, which was broken in two places. She put it in a splint, bandaged it up, and fastened it in a sling.

Like many of the survivors, Jack's father was exhausted. He needed to rest. Tomorrow, Jack would tell his father everything that had happened; for now, it was enough to know that he was all right. Jack sat beside him on the deck and watched him till he fell asleep. Then Jack got quietly to his feet and, nursing his injured arm, made his way over to Beryl to see if he could help.

Beryl and Quixote were winching the *Betsy II* on board and were deep in discussion about the best way to suspend it over the main deck. It was obvious they didn't need his help, so he went over to Dorothy.

The *Hyperion* was battle-scarred after her run-in with the *Nemesis*. She was still seaworthy, but there was a lot of work to do before they could begin their journey home. Eric Lamb and the engineer made a new mizzenmast from some of the *Belle*'s aluminum girders. The engineer was fascinated and pleased with the lightweight but sturdy material, and he disappeared below to use it to make some modifications to the engine.

Gadfly was put to work in the galley, where Mr. Treacle ran him ragged. Once they got to port, he would be handed over to the police, but until then, he had to work harder than he'd ever worked in his life, and he didn't like it.

By the late afternoon the *Hyperion* was ready to sail. Quixote gave the order for half steam astern and the ship backed slowly away from the ice. When they reached the wide channel where the *Nemesis* had gone down, Quixote brought the ship around and they were soon under way.

Once they were sailing in clear waters, Jack climbed up the companionway and joined Quixote at the rail. The captain was lost in thought. He was watching Beryl at work on her plane and a strange smile played across his face. Jack looked at Quixote. He was so different now. Jack couldn't imagine being afraid of this man. In fact, he'd almost forgotten that he'd ever felt that way.

Jack took the three rubies from his pocket and clinked them together in his hand. Quixote turned around.

"I thought . . . ," Jack began. "Well, I wanted to . . . to thank you. You know, for helping me . . . for taking me to find my father. Here," he said, holding out the rubies. "These are yours. You won them, remember?"

Quixote took the stones without a word. Jack started to move away.

"Wait," commanded Quixote. The captain carefully inspected each stone in turn. At last he seemed satisfied with them. He dropped two into his pocket, then lifted

Jack's hand and pressed the third stone into it. He rolled Jack's fingers closed.

"What's wrong with it?" Jack asked, opening his hand and gazing at the ruby.

"There's nothing wrong with it," replied Quixote. "Just take it. It's a thank-you present."

Jack frowned. Quixote leaned toward him.

"For giving me a proper challenge when I asked for one," he said. Then before Jack could say anything he turned on his heel and hurried down the companionway, leaving Jack alone.

Jack looked again at the ruby in his hand. It wasn't the largest of the three, but it was the most perfect. He slipped it into his pocket and smiled.

The next day Jack sat by his father's side. An uncomfortable silence yawned between them. Jack knew that he had to tell his father what had happened, but he didn't know how to begin. His father would be so angry. Jack glanced once or twice at the steel gray eyes with their unfathomable expression, then looked away.

"I knew as I was climbing the ladder that I shouldn't," Jack began. "I knew I was breaking my promise to you. But the air shaft was there and there was no one around and I just wanted to look out at the clouds. That was all. I know it was wrong and I know I'll be punished, perhaps even court-martialed, for what I did, but I just wanted you to know that I was sorry."

"Jack," Captain Black said, gently lifting his son's chin. Jack looked up and saw a curious warmth in the eyes he'd thought so cold. "I know you're sorry, and I know you can see it was wrong to disobey an order, and even worse to break a promise. I hope that you'll never break your word again, but I am so proud of you. You have been so brave. You believed you could find us and you never gave up."

Captain Black sighed.

"When Keats came and told me that you'd fallen off the airship, I was beside myself. Gadfly volunteered to fly off and search for your body in the sea. Search for your body . . ." Jack's father turned his face toward the sky. "And then, when the bomb went off . . ."

"Was it very bad?" Jack asked.

His father nodded. "I was in the control room when I felt a shudder run through the *Belle*. I looked out and saw the tail fin floating down toward the water, just drifting, swish-swaying . . ." He made a motion with his hand. "Like a leaf on a breeze.

"With the tail fin gone, the airship shot straight up into the sky. Anything that wasn't nailed down in the control car smashed through the windows and fell out to the ice. We lost a lot of our instruments that way. You see, Jack, if you hadn't climbed up the air shaft and taken that reading, and kept hold of that sextant, we might never have been found. I'm not saying what you did was right, but if you hadn't done it . . . well . . ."

"But how did you land?"

"I had to get the men to act as human ballast. They were terrific. First they climbed up into the nose and then, once their weight brought the nose down and we were on an even keel, they spread themselves out along the length of the gangway to keep her stable. We knew we couldn't hold her like that forever. We didn't have much time, so we brought her down as smoothly as we could. Men hung from the girders, carefully shifting their weight to where it was needed. We vented gas to lower the airship. And the one thought in my head was 'It doesn't matter if we have no gas, it'll be all right. We just have to get to the ground safely. Gadfly will go for help.' We did the best we could, and although we hit the ice like a brick, almost all of us survived the crash. Then we had to sit on the ice and hope we'd survive till someone rescued us. We didn't know then how far off course we were."

Jack marveled at his father. Obviously, his skill and cool head had saved the *Belle*, but he didn't boast about it, as Gadfly would have done. Instead, he told of everyone's part in the affair, not just his own.

"What will happen to Gadfly?" asked Jack.

"He will be court-martialed," his father replied sadly. "But let's not think about him now. I don't want to spoil how happy I am to be here with you." Then he smiled at

Jack and it was like the sun coming out from behind a cloud. Jack loved the way his father smiled.

The days that followed were the happiest of Jack's life. He and his father spent all their time together talking and playing long games of gin rummy or just sitting quietly side by side. Jack was utterly and blissfully happy.

With each day that passed the weather became warmer and the men from the airship grew stronger. Fair winds carried the *Hyperion* south across calm seas. In the evenings, Thomas and Horatio sang together to entertain the men from the airship. They sang funny songs and sad songs, and songs that made the men long for home, but they never once sang the song that Jack had heard them sing in their sleep; perhaps it was too special to them.

On the third day of their voyage the wind dropped and the *Hyperion* bobbed in a dead calm sea. Quixote, tearing himself away from Beryl, was about to call for the engines when Sky suddenly cried from the crosstrees, "Captain . . . Off the port stern, Captain!"

Quixote leaped up the companionway and onto the poop deck. He hurried to the rail. A little way off the stern bubbled a vast circle of white water.

"Everyone to the lifelines," he bellowed as the monster's huge head rose out of the sea.

Dorothy, Sky, and Jack ran about the deck making sure that all the sick men were secured to something. Jack and his father held on to a lifeline. The crew clung to the shrouds.

With her head out of the water the sea monster wailed and lifted her enormous flippers high.

"Hold on, everybody!" cried Quixote, grabbing hold of the wheel. "Let's see if we can get her to take us all the way home."

The monster brought her flippers down and the ship rode the enormous wave. She howled and chased after the ship, making wave after wave. By the evening the *Hyperion* had traveled farther than she had in the past three days. As the moon rose, Sky called out, "Land to starboard, Captain."

Behind the ship the monster rose once more, but Quixote commanded her not to splash, and the monster, being a little worn out, sank obediently beneath the waves.

Those who could rushed over to the starboard rail and gazed at the twinkling lights along the dark hillside.

"Land," whispered Sky.

"A town," said the Fell twins together.

"Houses," sighed Eric Lamb as he gazed at the lights.

"Home," said Mr. Treacle as he smiled and threw his almost full flagon of syrup into the sea.

The twins looked at each other and began to sing the song that Jack had only ever heard them sing in their sleep.

My love is like a red, red rose
That's newly sprung in June.
My love is like a melody
That's sweetly sung in tune.

Quixote and Beryl stood at the rail listening to the Fell twins' song as it floated across the night.

As fair art thou, my bonnie lass,
So deep in love am I.
And I will love thee still, my dear,
Till a' the seas gang dry.

When the song was finished, Quixote came over to Jack and Captain Black. The harbor lights sparkled across the water and welcomed them in.

"We'll take you as close to the harbor as we can, Captain Black, if that's all right, and we'll call for boats to come and fetch you."

"Won't you come with us, Captain Quixote?" asked Jack's father. "You and your men would be most welcome to stay in our house, and it would be an honor for me to return your hospitality."

Quixote shook his head. "I can't speak for my men, they can go where they choose, but I don't think there's anything for me on land. Though I would dearly love to see one of your airships."

"Maybe you will one day, if you're lucky," said Beryl as she joined them. She smiled at Jack and his father, but Quixote didn't turn to greet her.

"I suppose you'll want to get your plane down soon," said Quixote. He was silent for some time, then turned and looked at her. "You know you could always sail around the world with . . ."

All at once there was a horrible crunching sound from the front of the ship. Quixote grabbed a long-handled oar and raced to the prow. The monster had sneaked under the ship and was once more happily sharpening her teeth on the wooden hull.

"To the pumps!" Quixote cried, holding the oar high above his head. The monster backed away and sank with one last plaintive howl. Quixote quickly surveyed the damage. "She's chewed out half the frame. We're taking on water fast. Get pumping. Eric, quick, take us into port."

When the crew of the *Hyperion* heard Quixote's order, they gave a great cheer. They were going home at last.

By the time they reached the port, the *Hyperion* was listing badly in the water. She was a good deal less than seaworthy. The port was only a small fishing town, and when they saw the damaged ship come in, the townsfolk hurried out of their houses to see if they could help.

When everyone was off the ship and installed in the warm kitchens of the townsfolk, and Gadfly was lying on a bunk in the cell of the local police station, Jack stood with his father and Beryl and Dorothy on the dock while Quixote held up a lamp to see the damage to the *Hyperion*'s prow. It was bad. The huge gaping hole yawned at them.

"We could always *fly* around the world, if you'd like." Beryl's eyes sparkled. "If you want a bit of a challenge, that is."

Quixote looked at her and they both started to laugh.

"What will you do, Dorothy?" asked Jack, leaving Beryl and Quixote on their own. "Will you come and stay with us?"

"Well," began Dorothy, holding on to Nelson's paws to stop him from pulling at her hair, "I was wanting to ask your father about that. I never thought there was much for an old woman to do back home. They're usually put out to pasture like old workhorses, and I've never been able to stomach the idea of that. But ever since I saw Beryl's plane, I've had a hankering to try my hand at it. It just looks like so much fun. What do you say, Captain Black? Will you teach me to fly?"

"It would be an honor," answered Jack's father with a

slight bow. "But you'll have to wait your turn. You see, I'm going to be rather busy giving my son his first flying lessons."

Jack couldn't believe his ears. "Do you mean it? You'll teach me to fly? You'll really teach me to fly?"

Captain Black nodded. Jack grabbed his father's hand and shook it vigorously.

"Thank you," he said, grinning broadly. "Thank you so much."

Jack was so excited that he howled with joy and ran along the quay toward the town, with his one good arm outstretched like the wing of a plane.